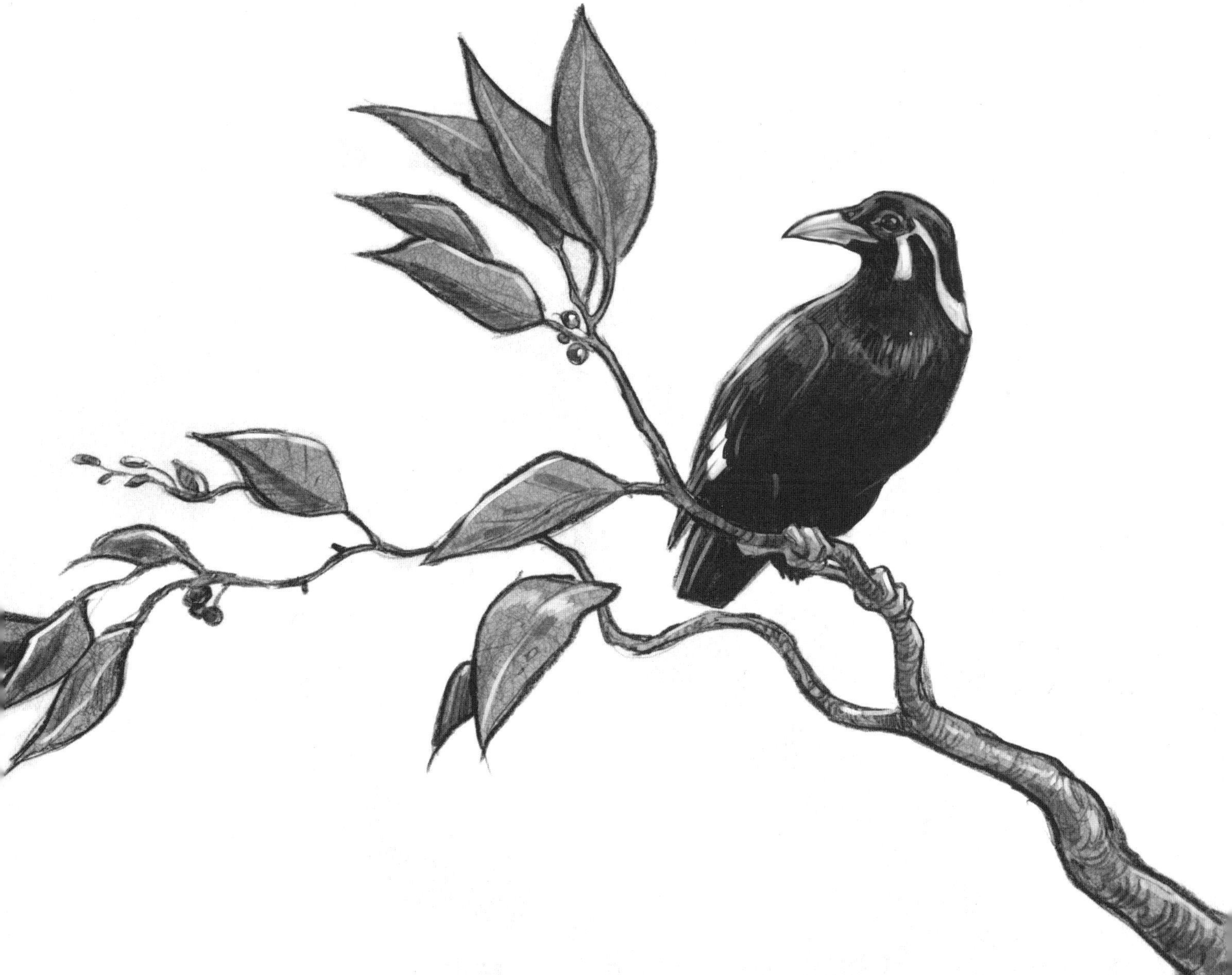

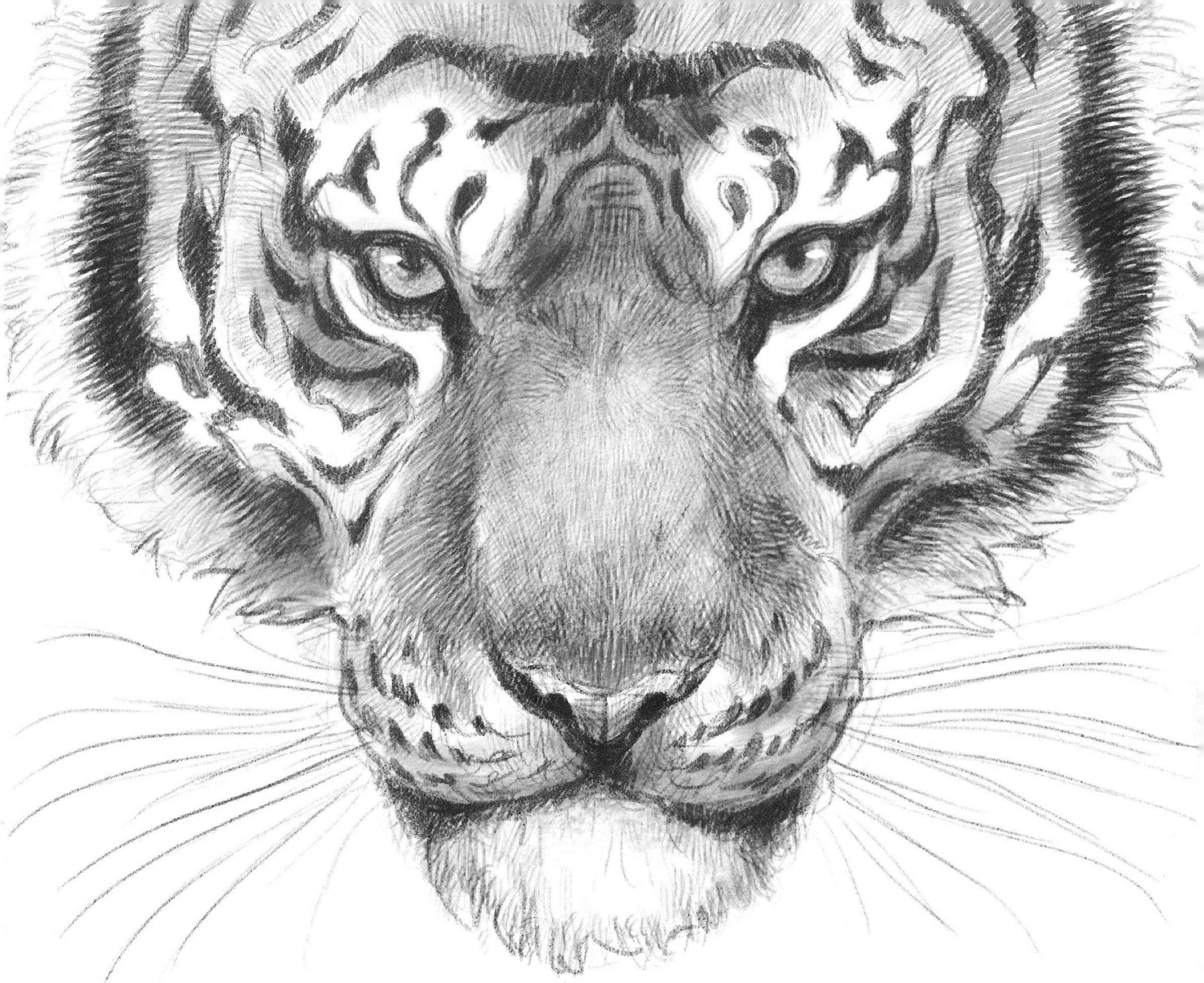

Love

THE TIGER

Frédéric Brrémaud
Federico Bertolucci

MAGNETICPRESS
www.MAGNETIC-PRESS.com

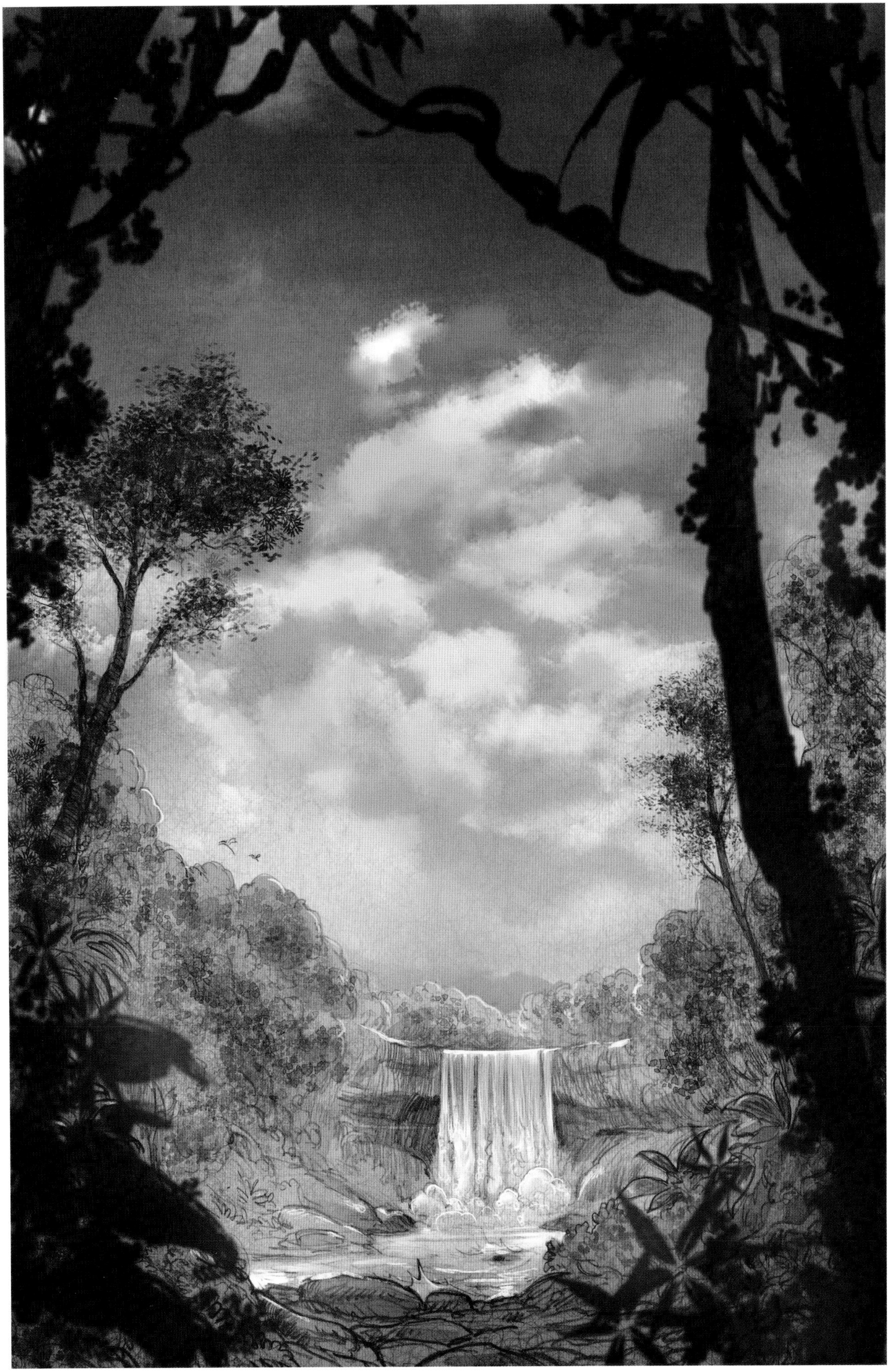

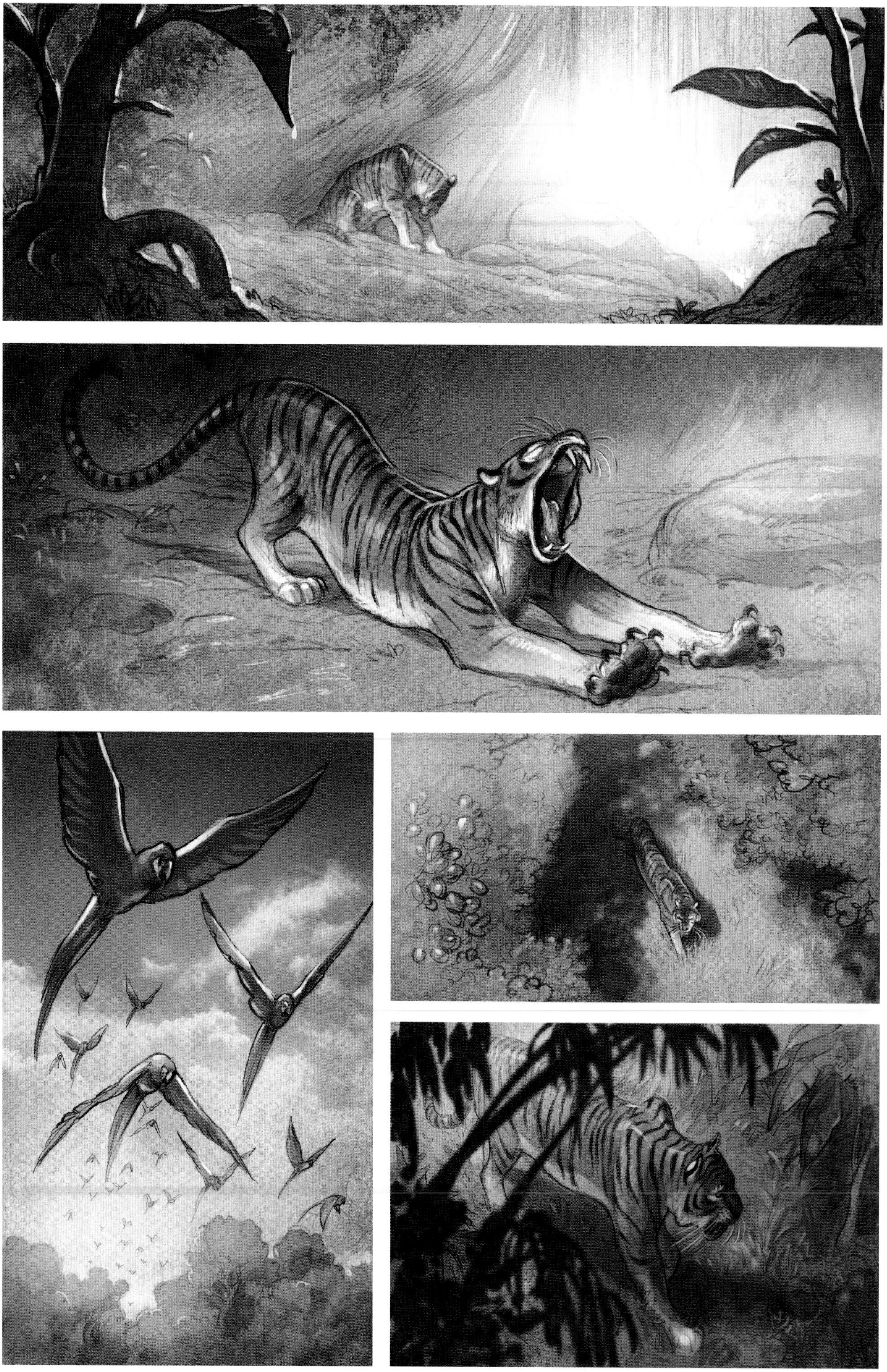

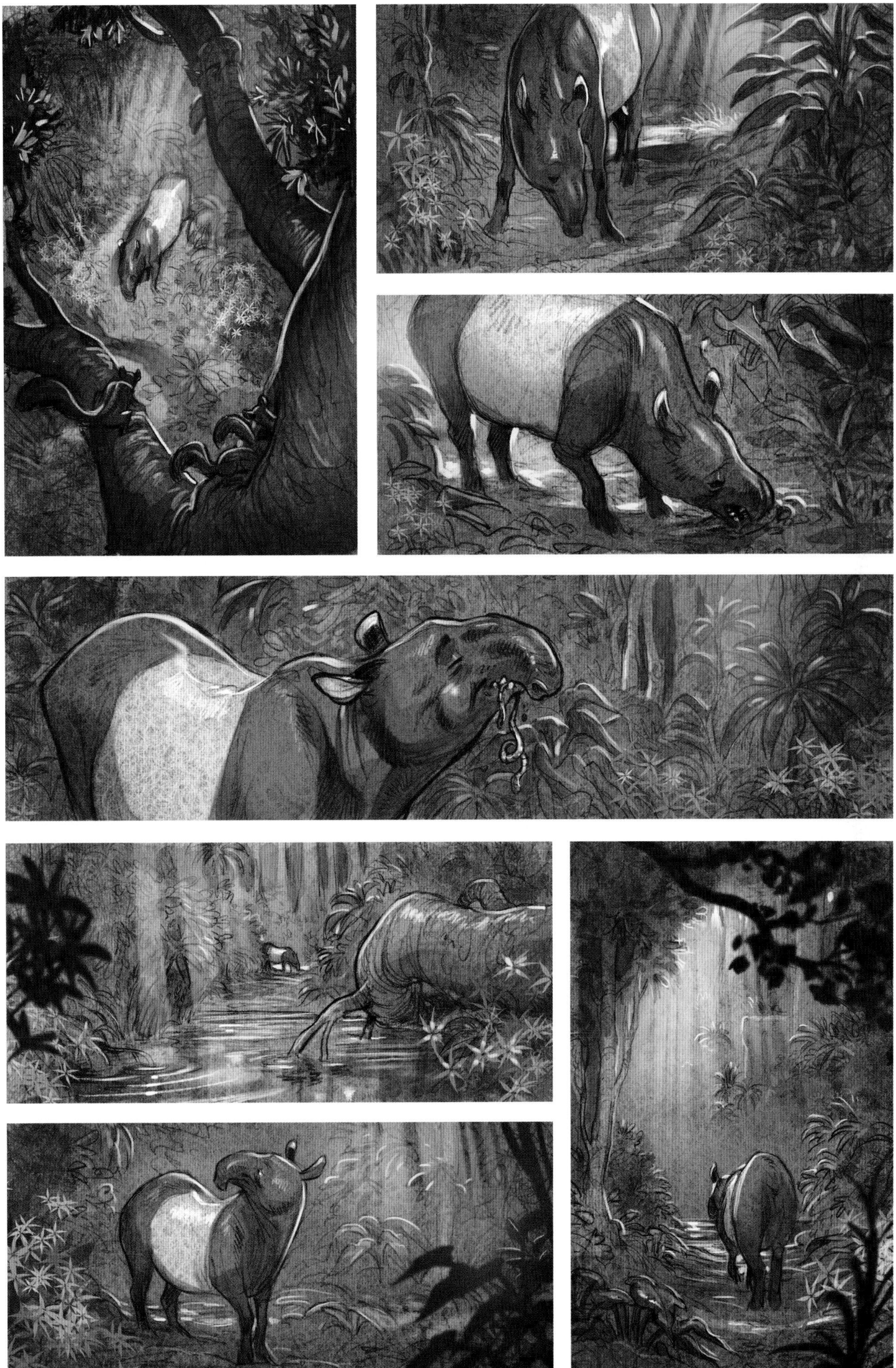

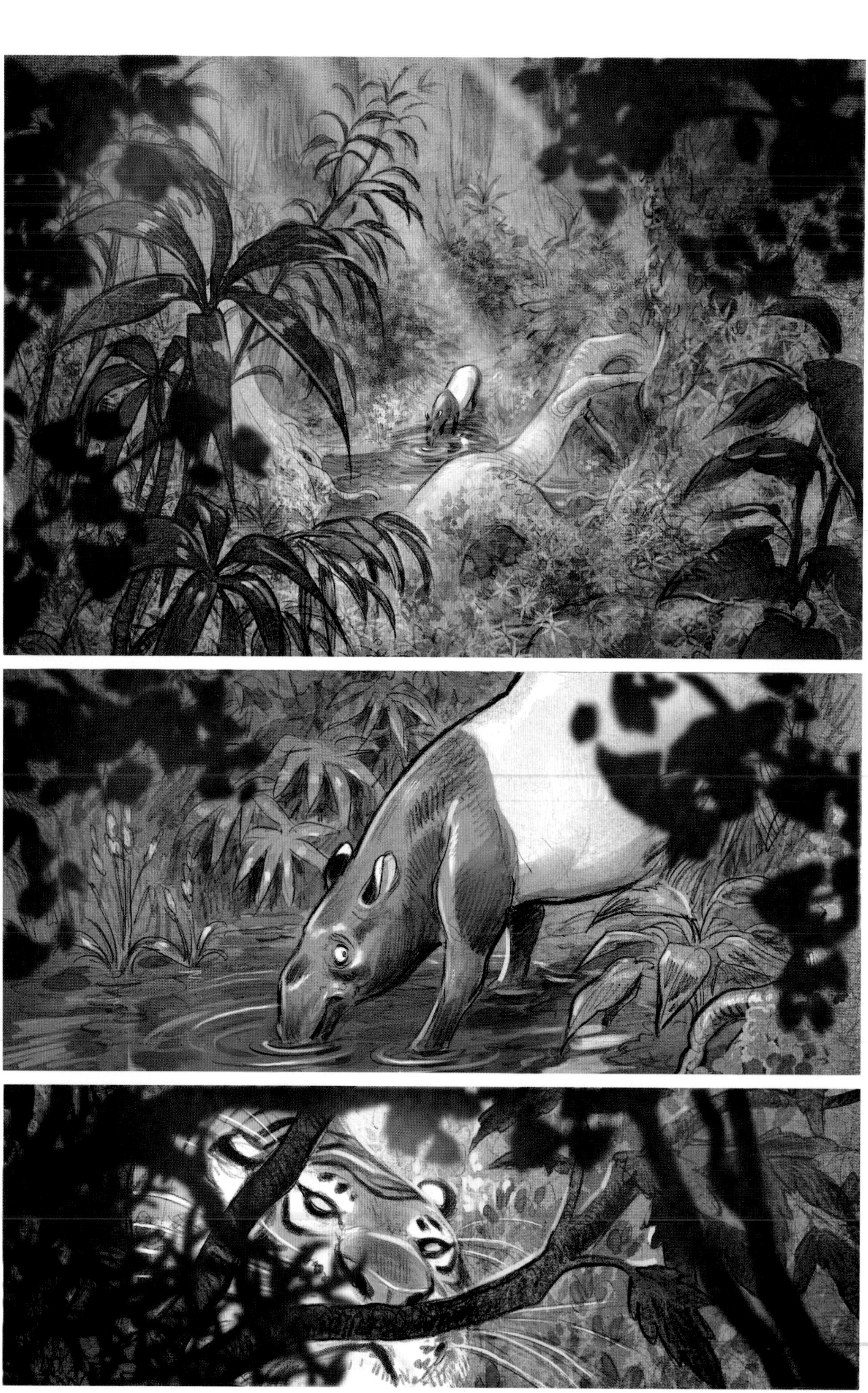

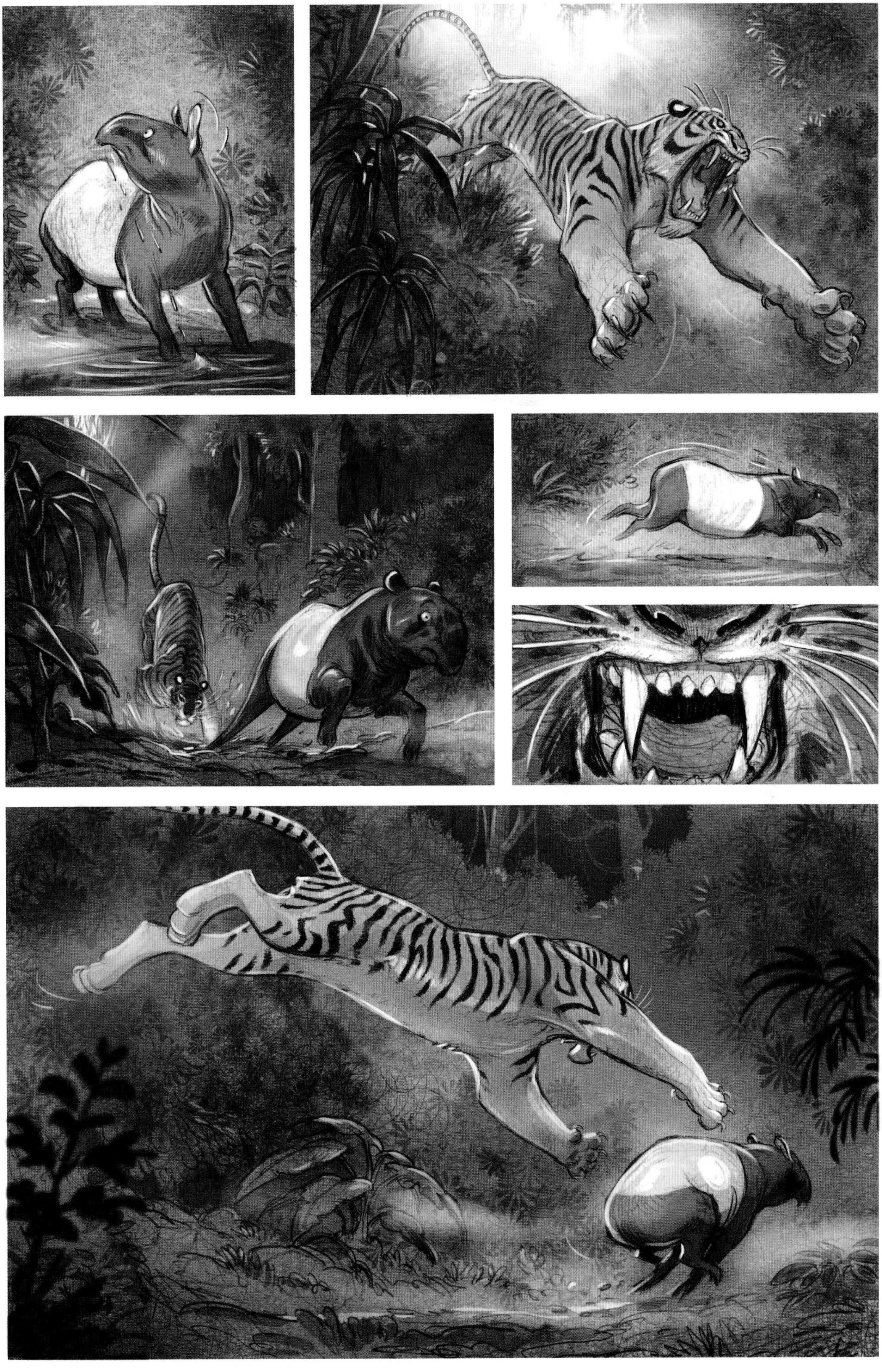

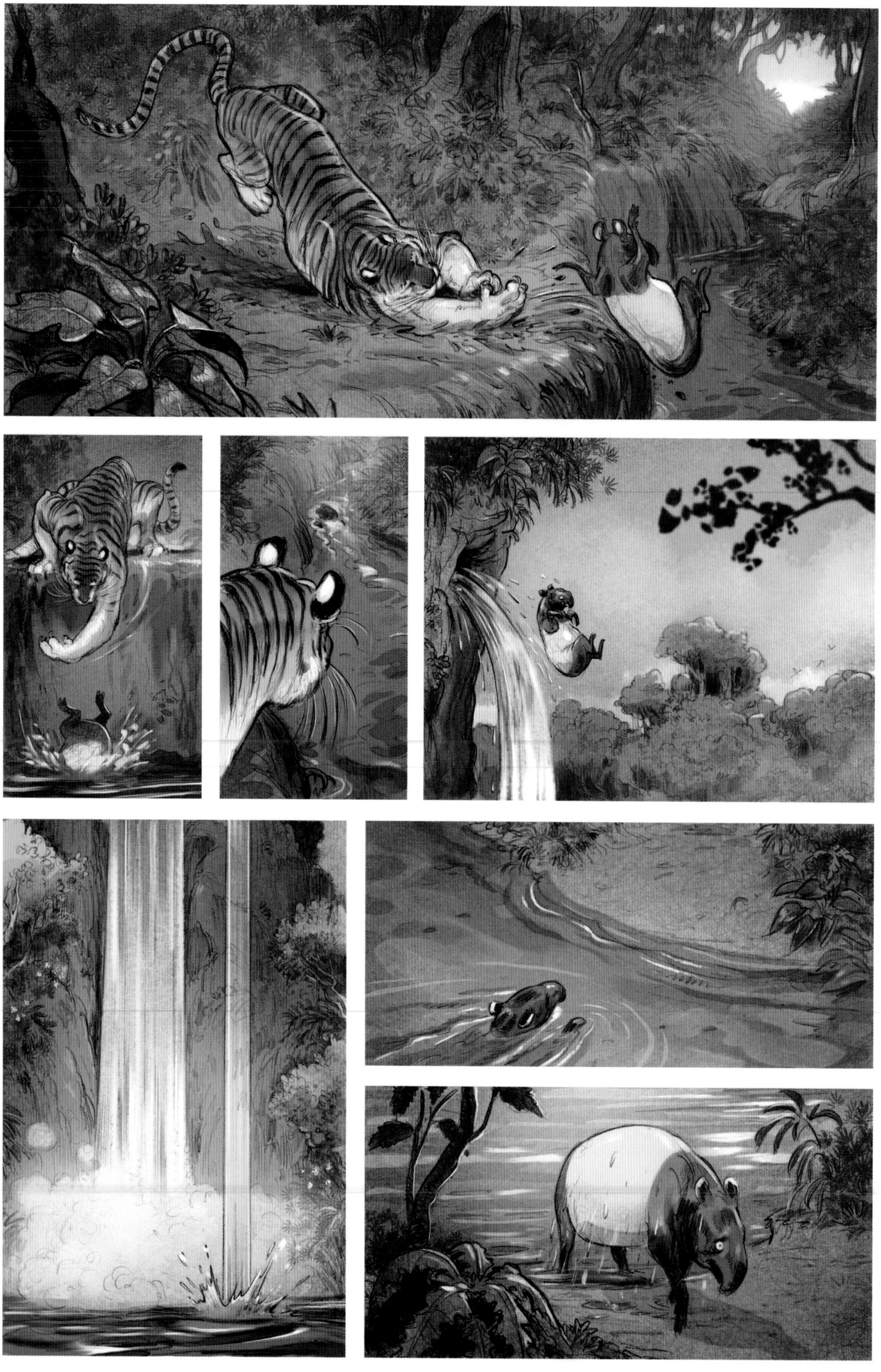

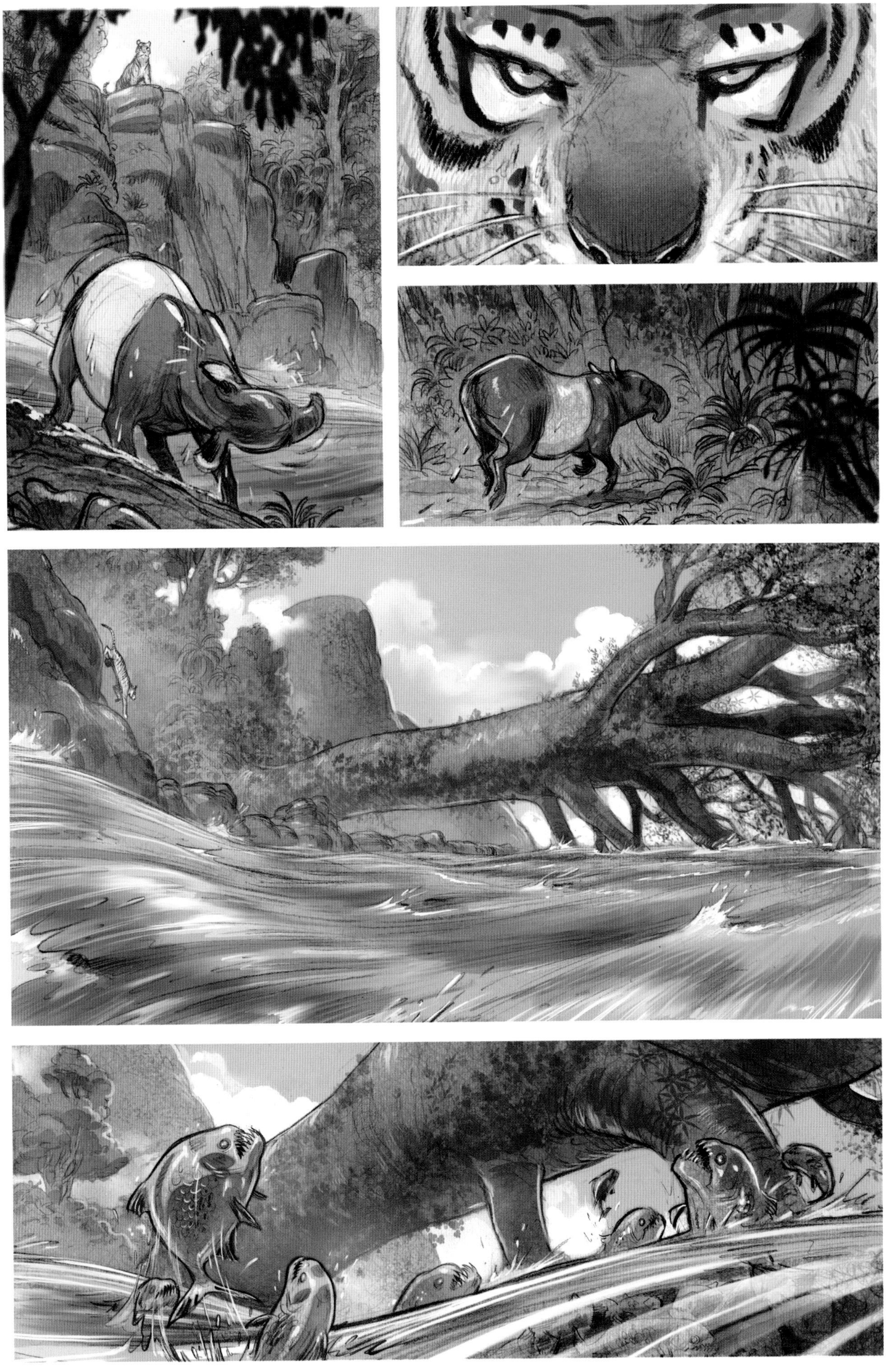

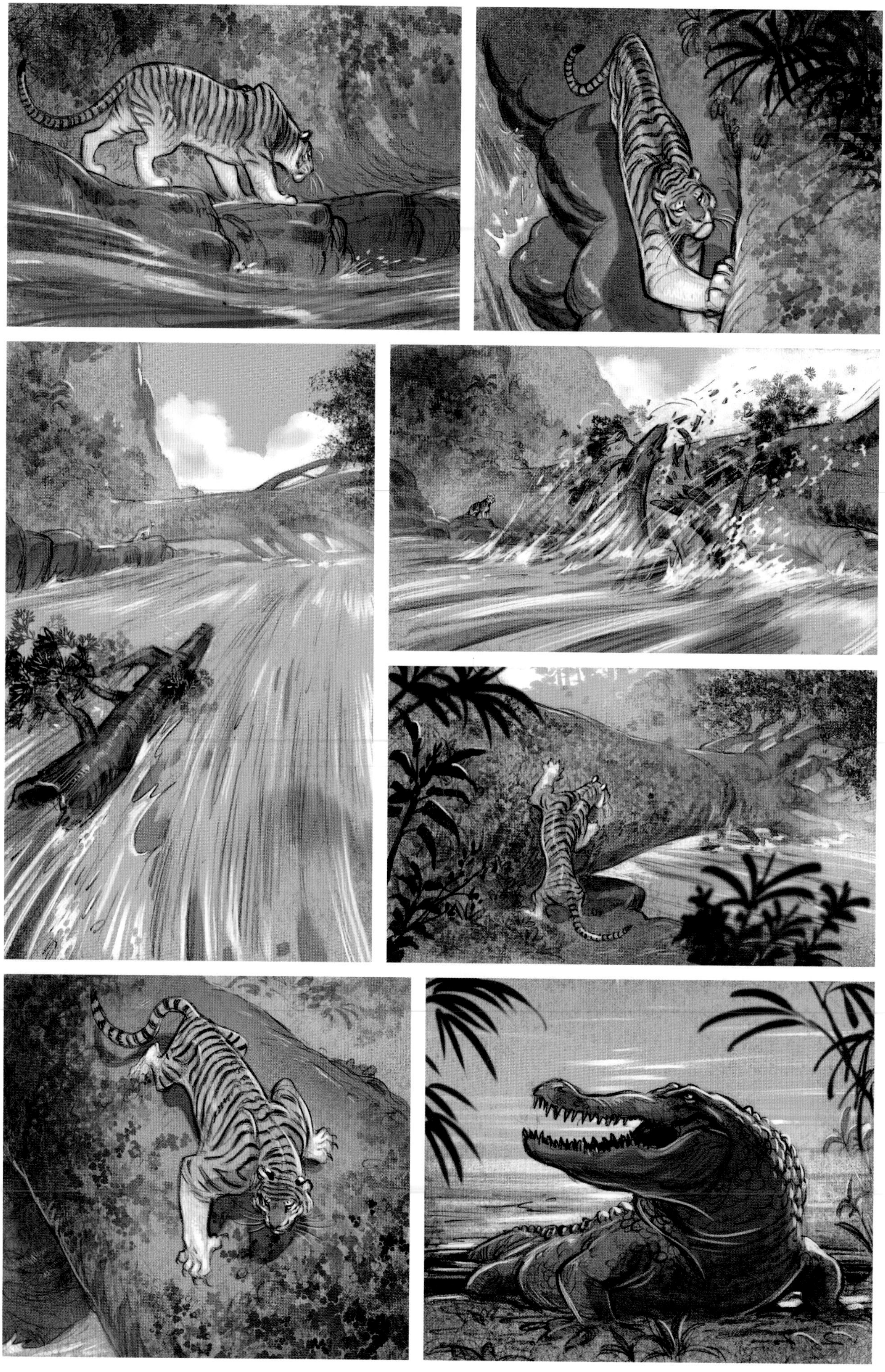

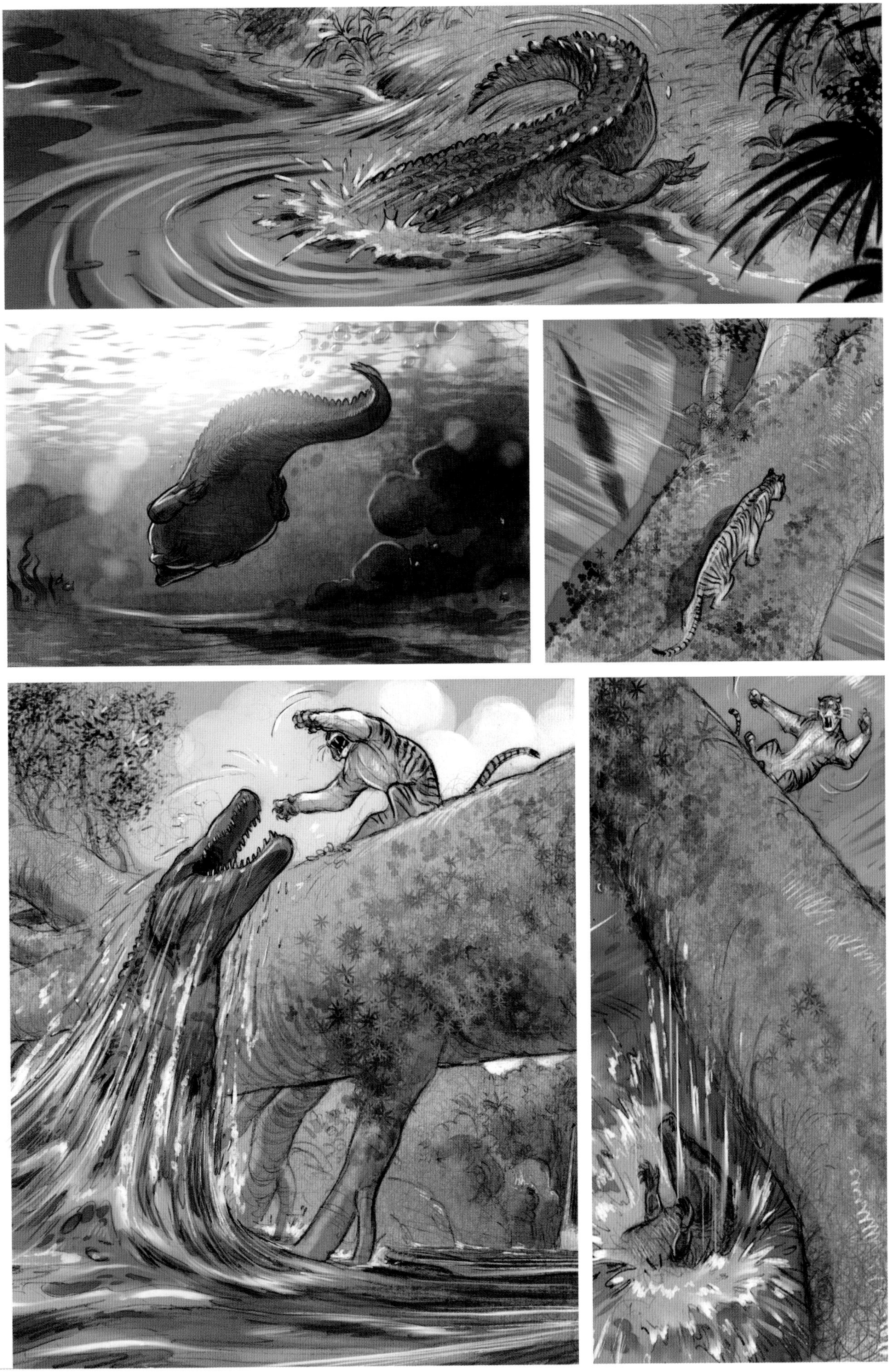

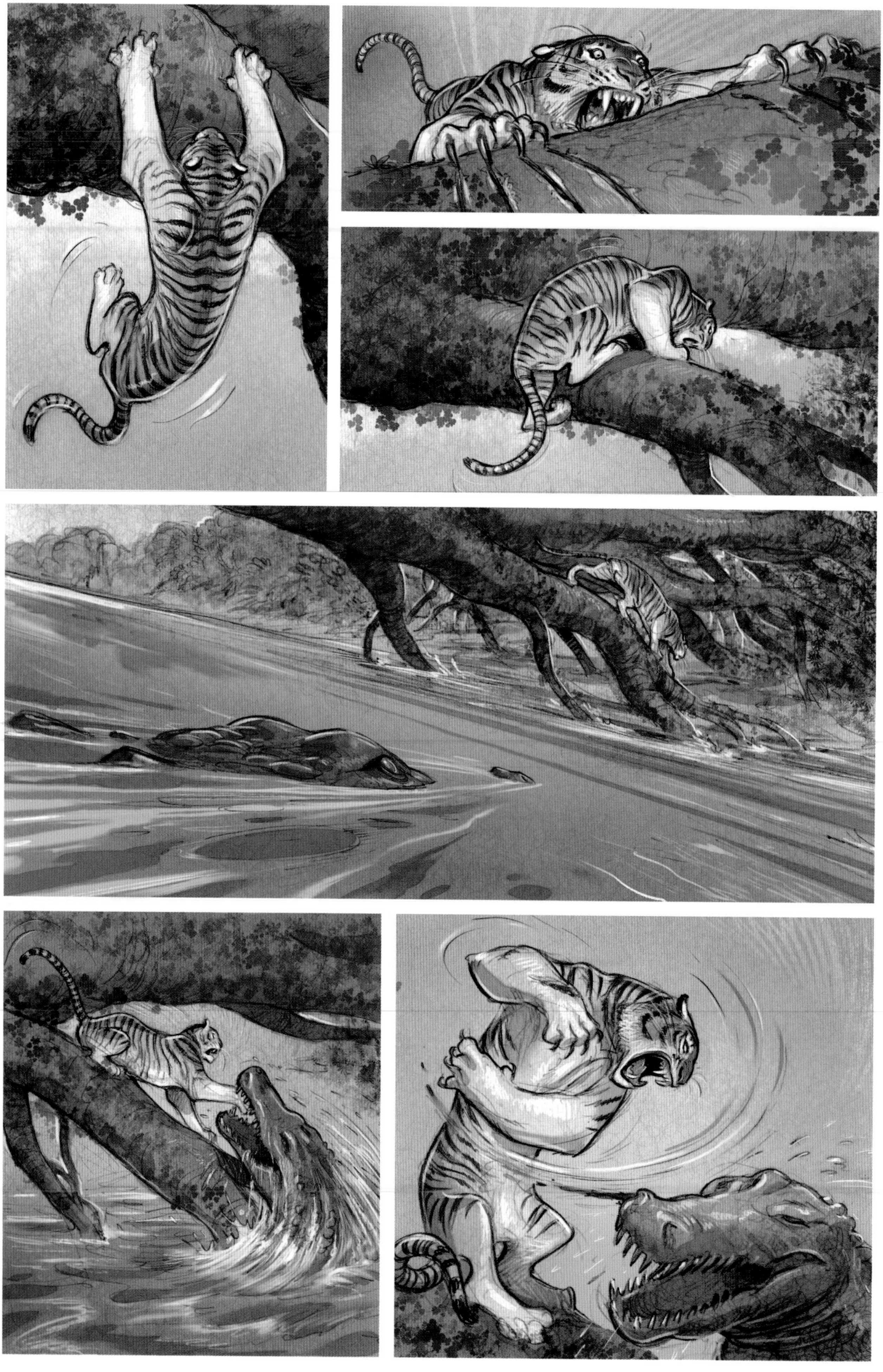

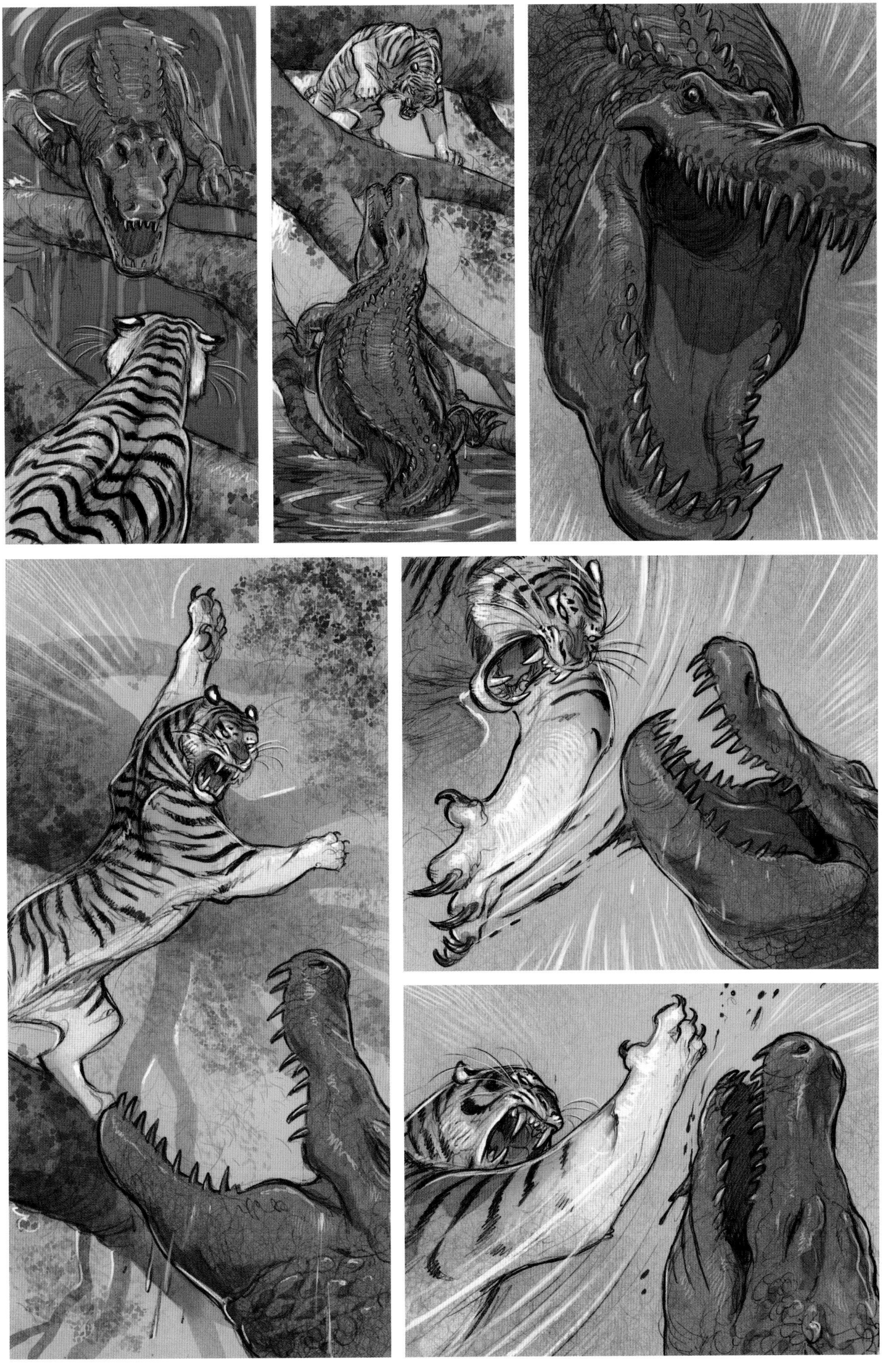

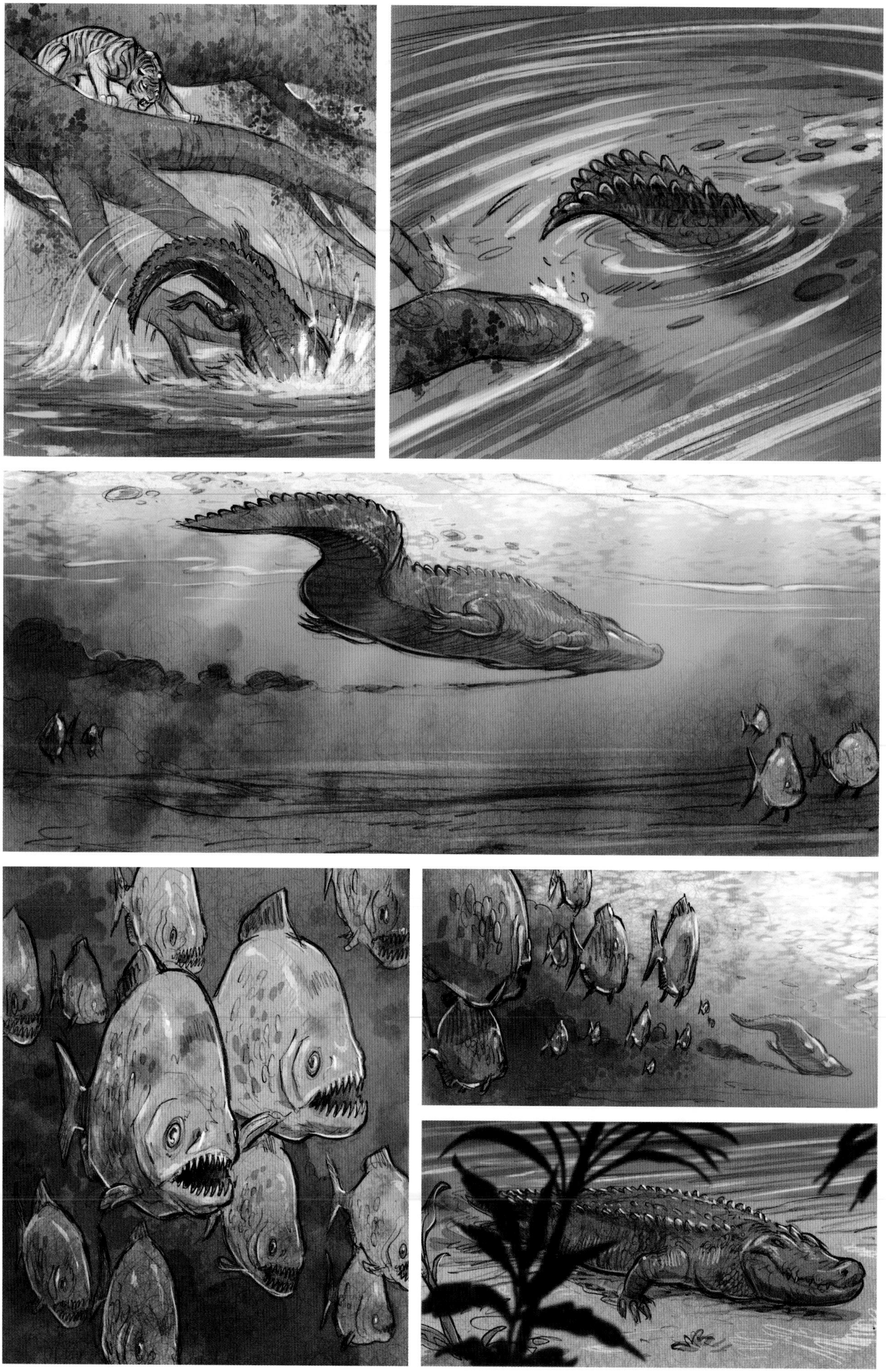

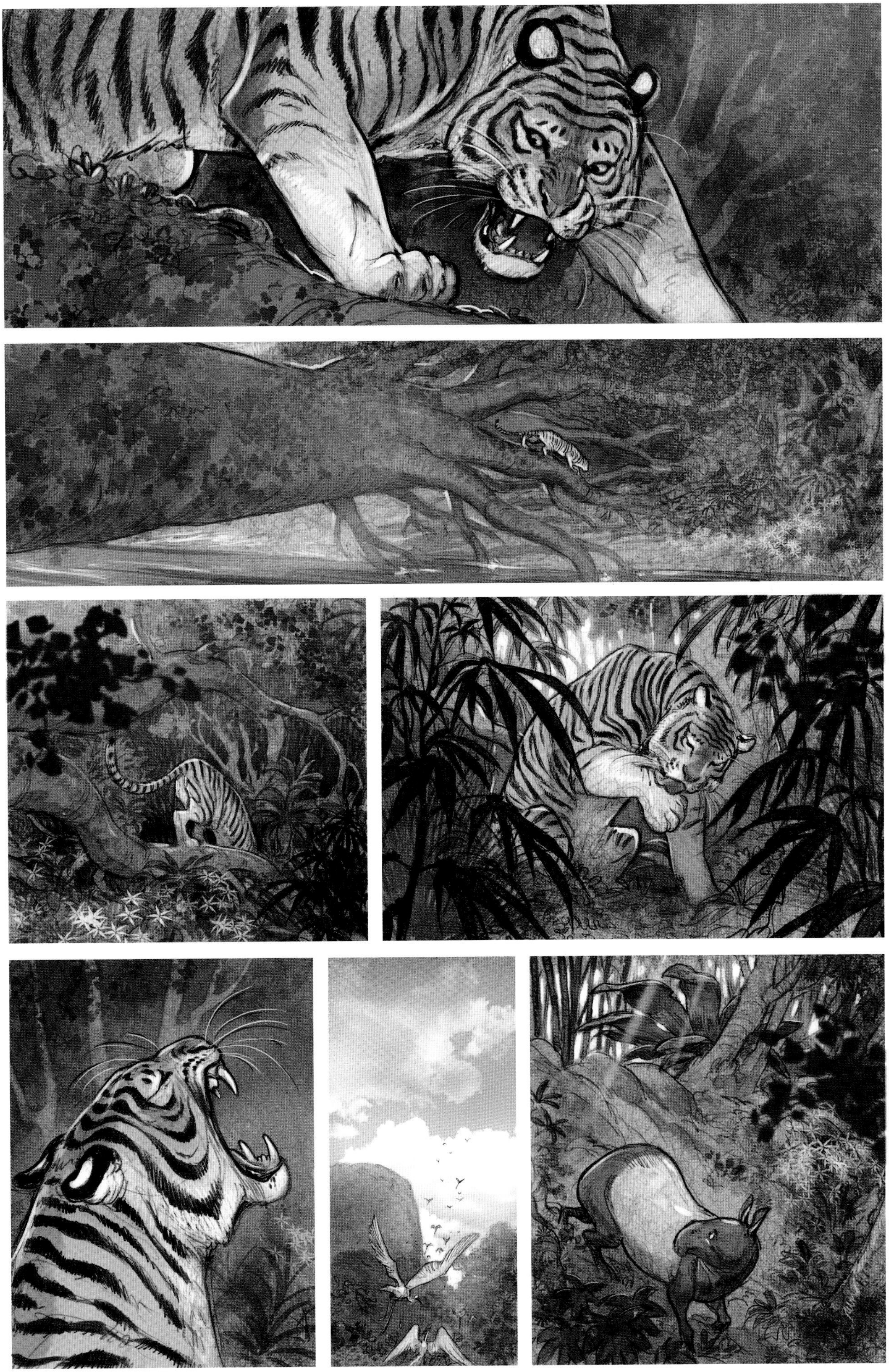

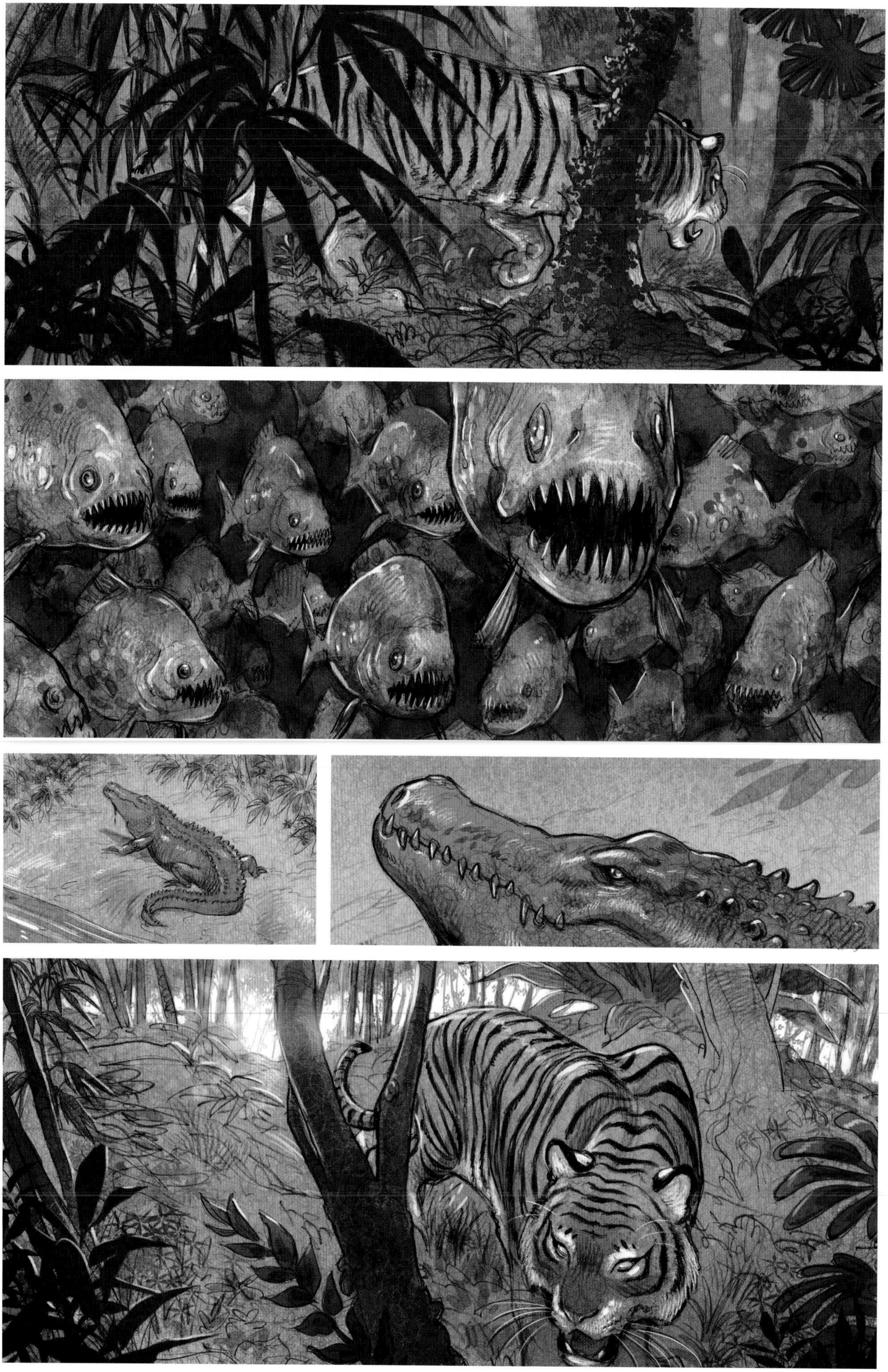

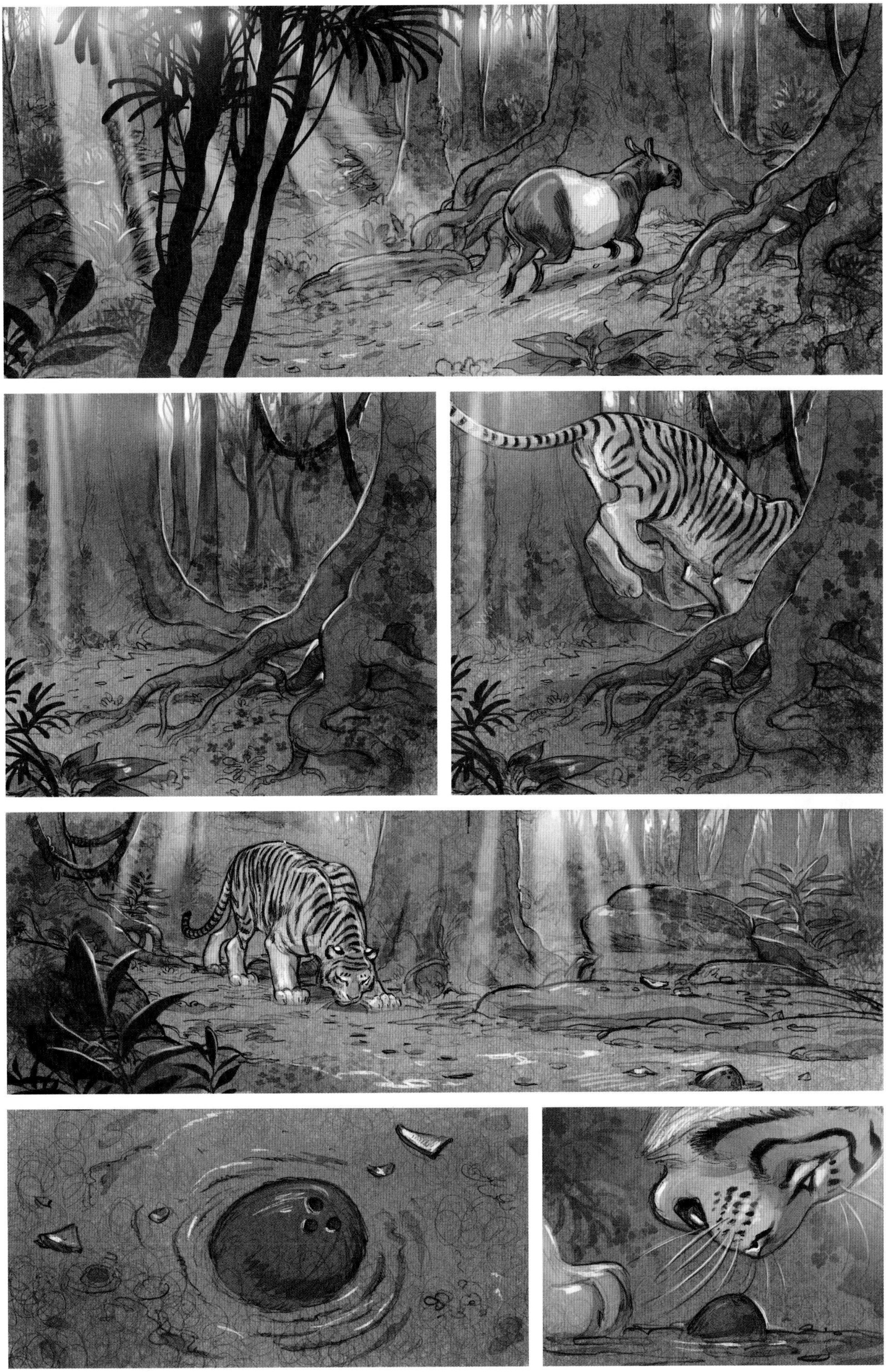

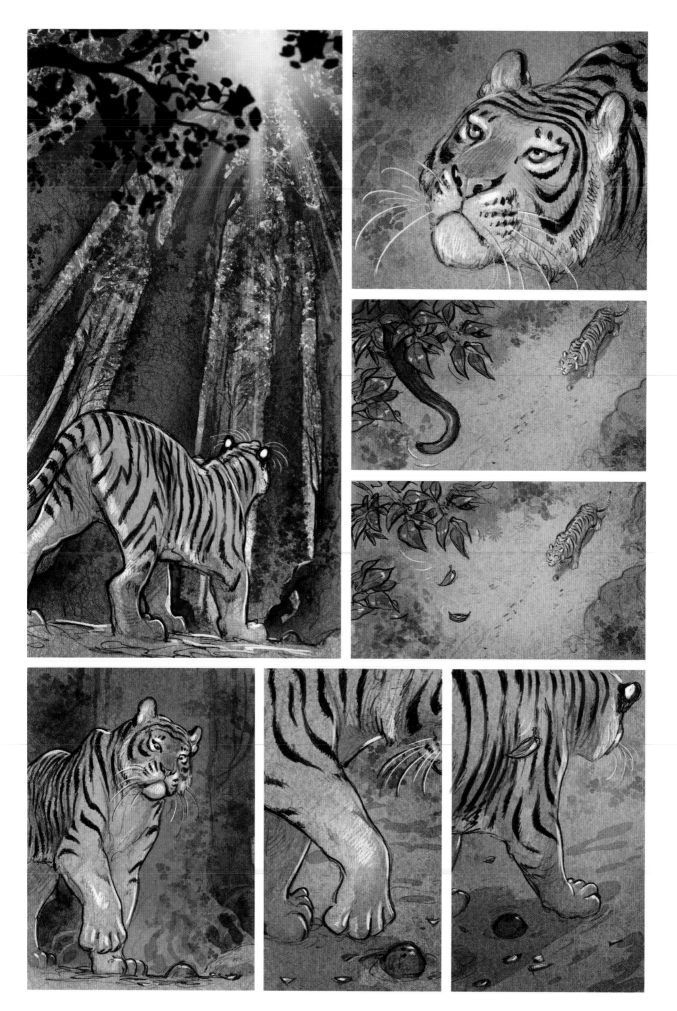

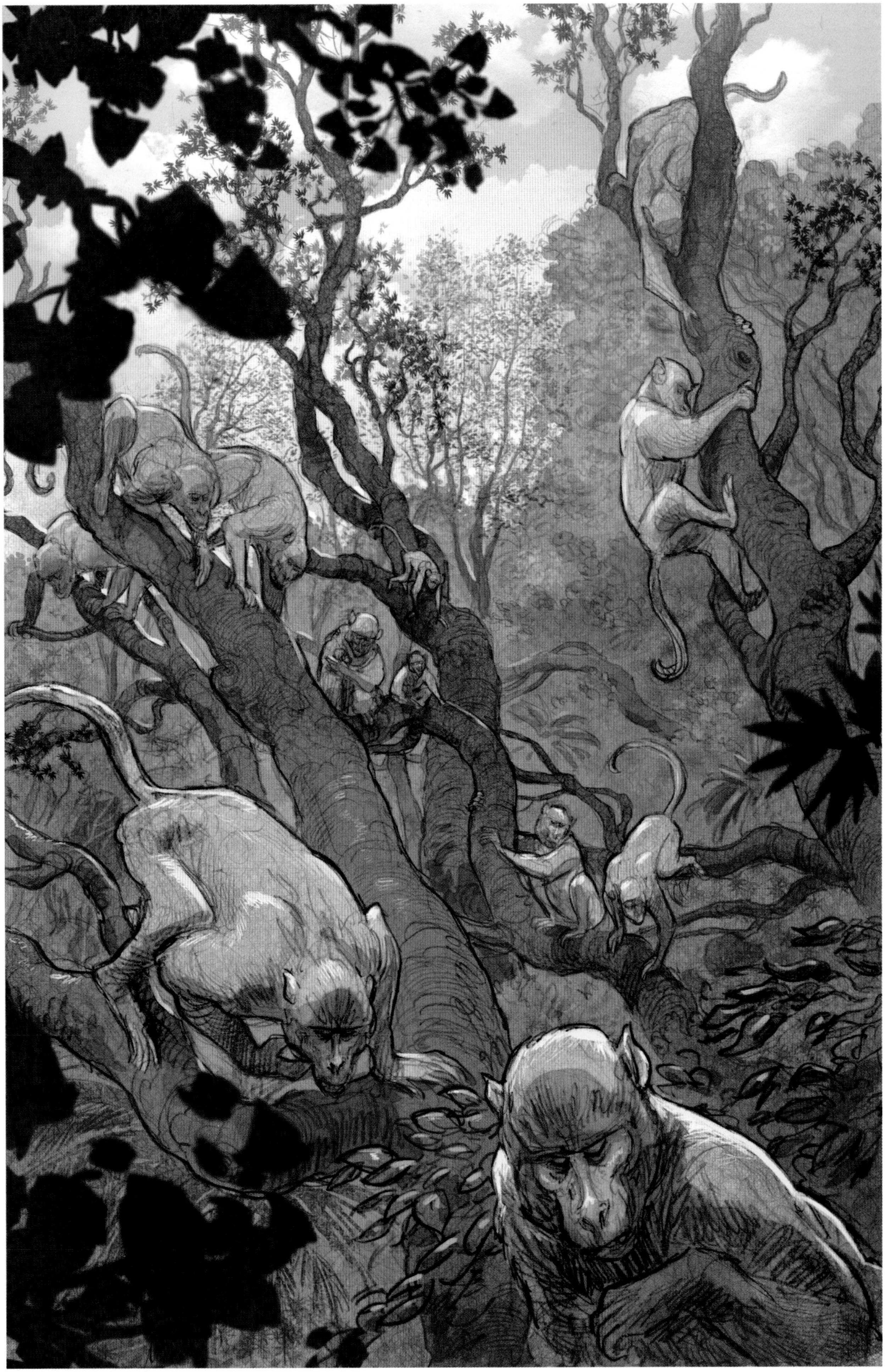

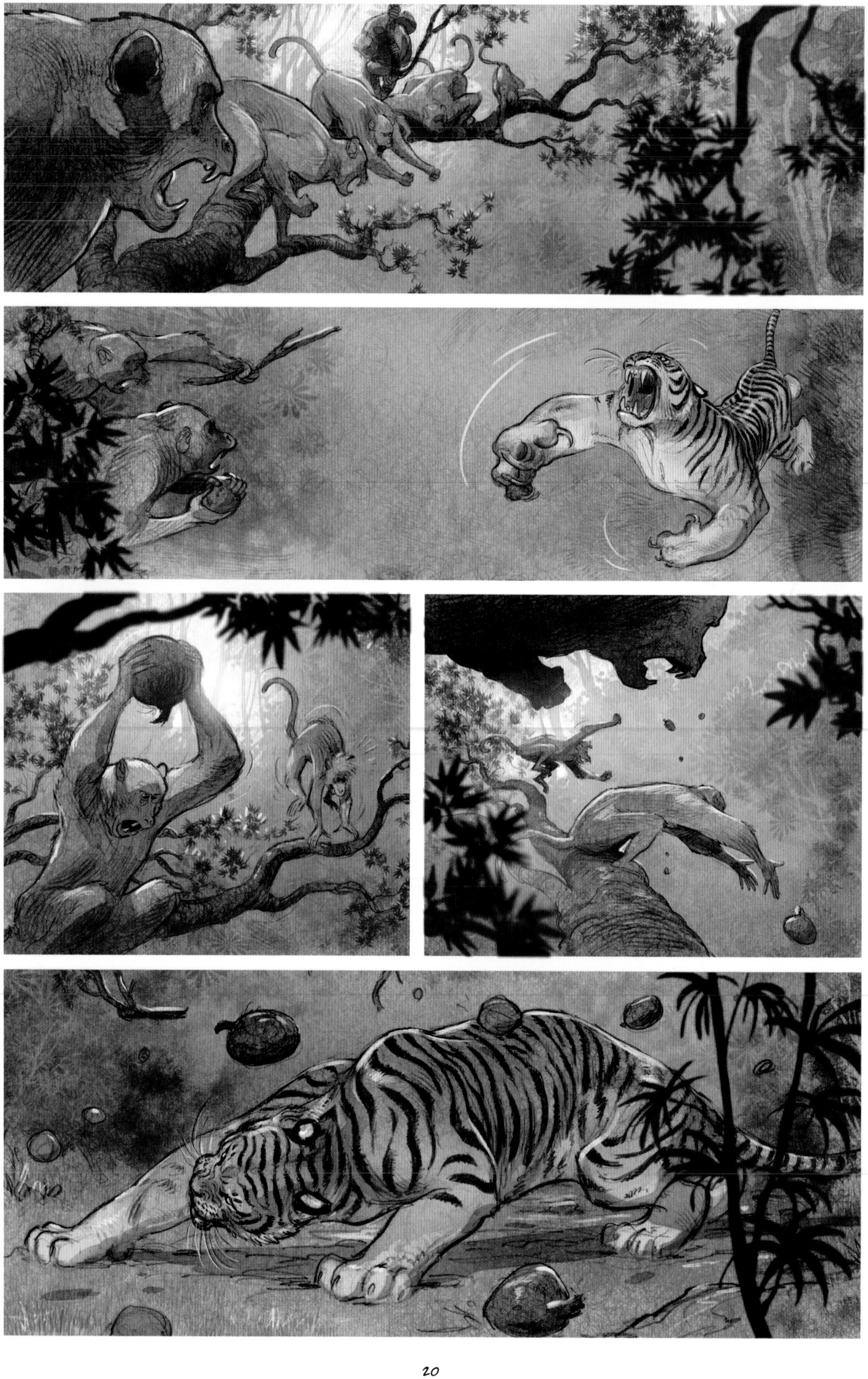

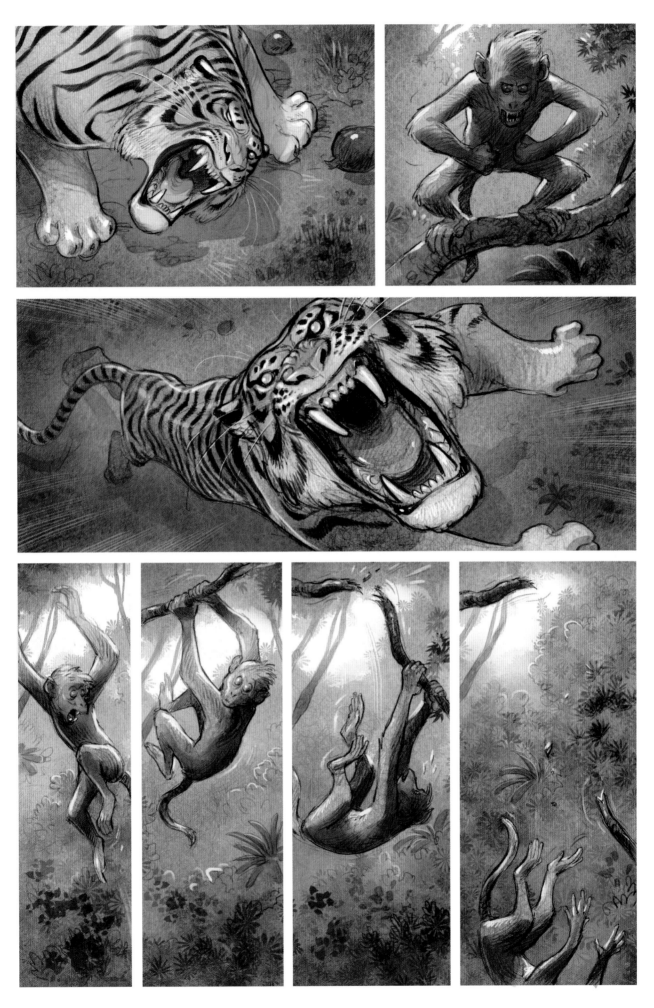

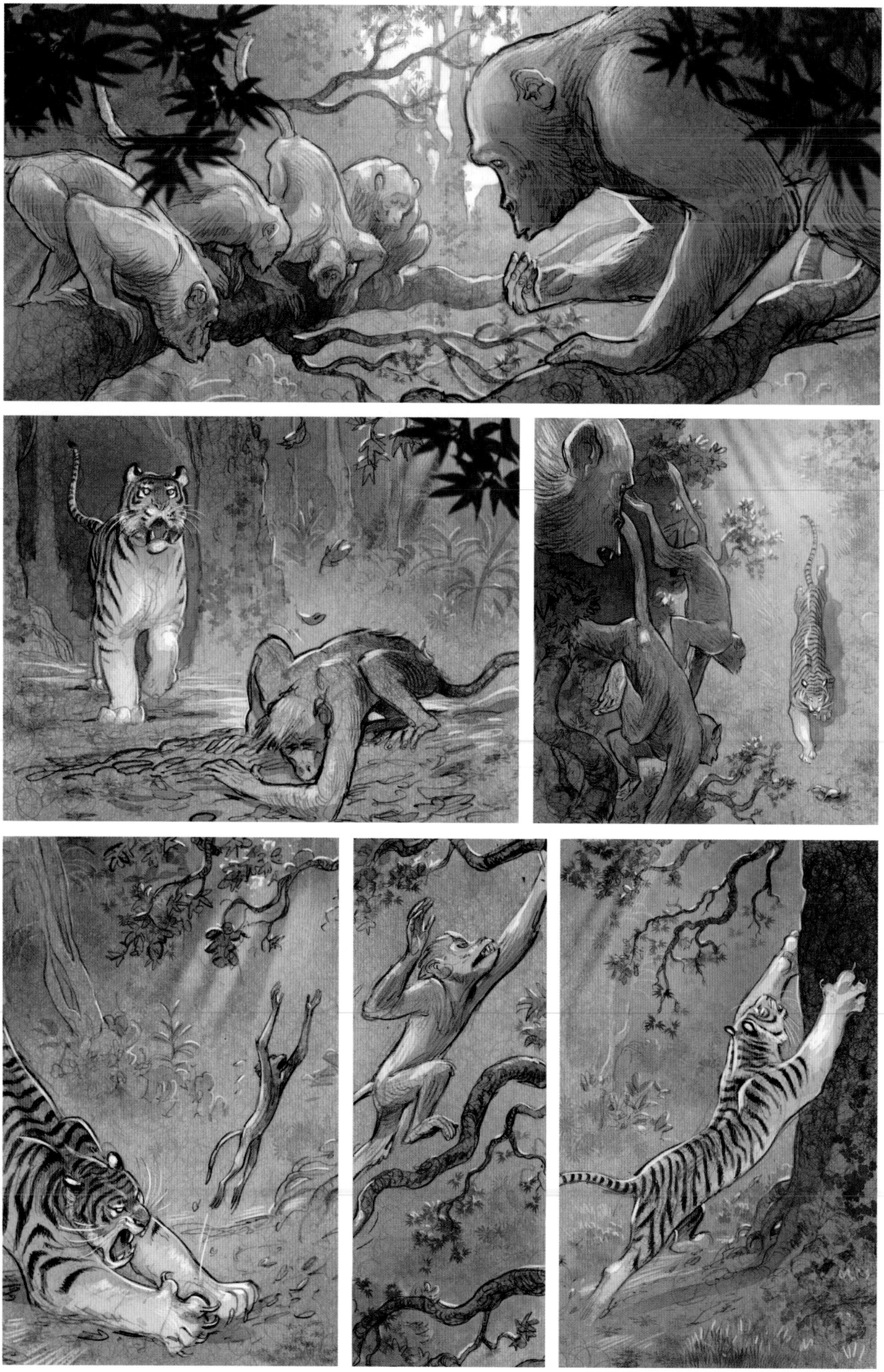

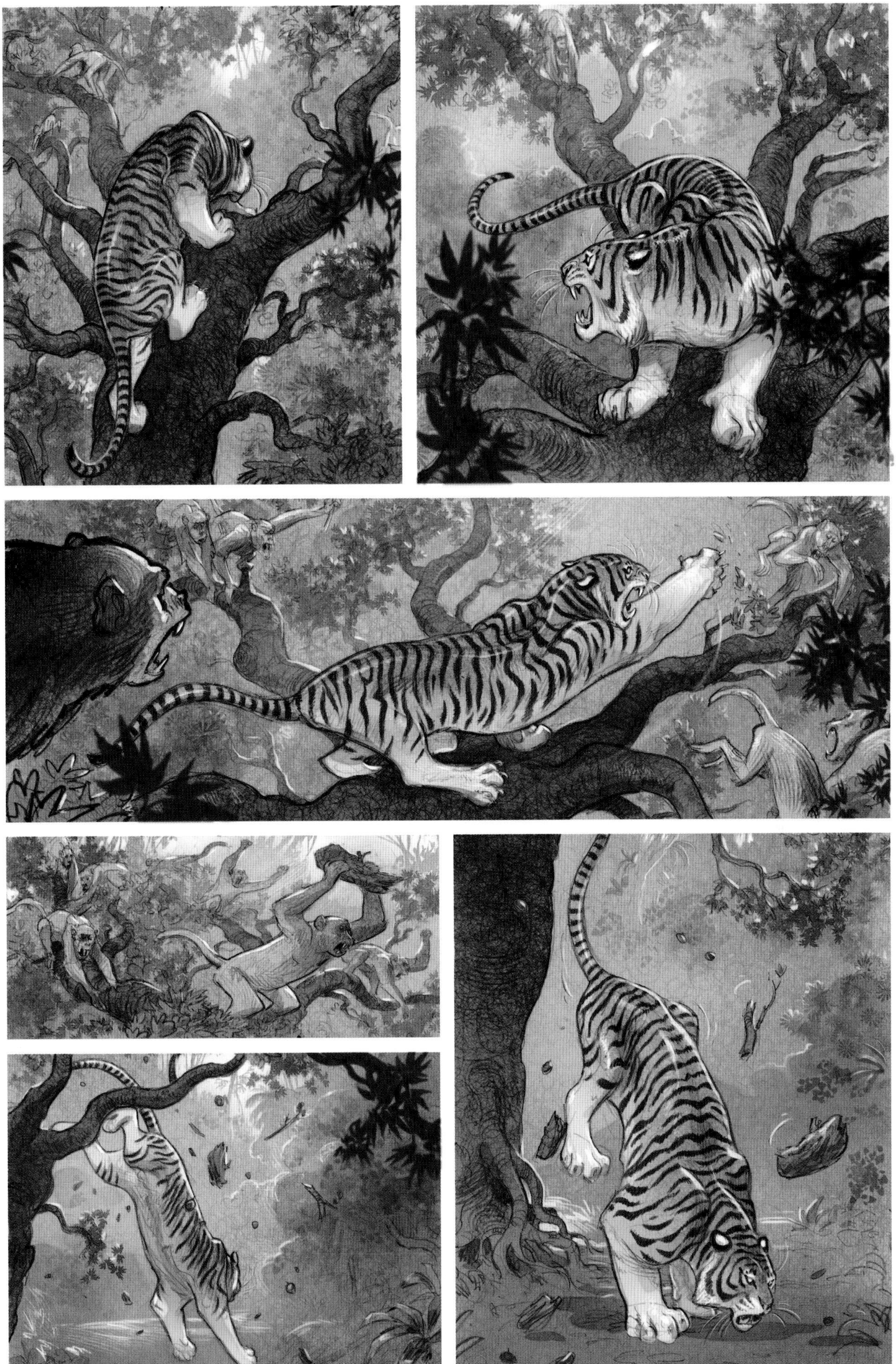

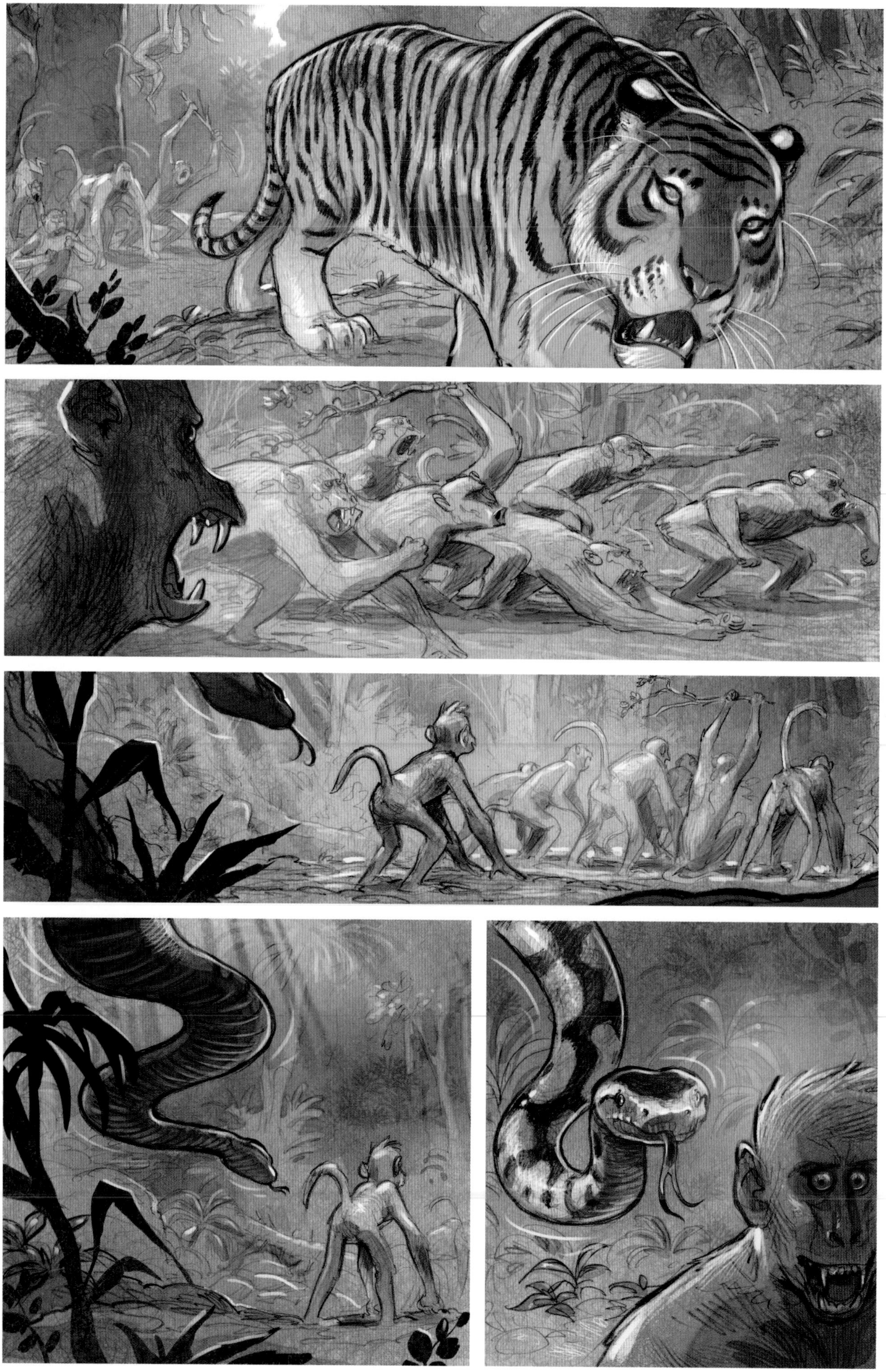

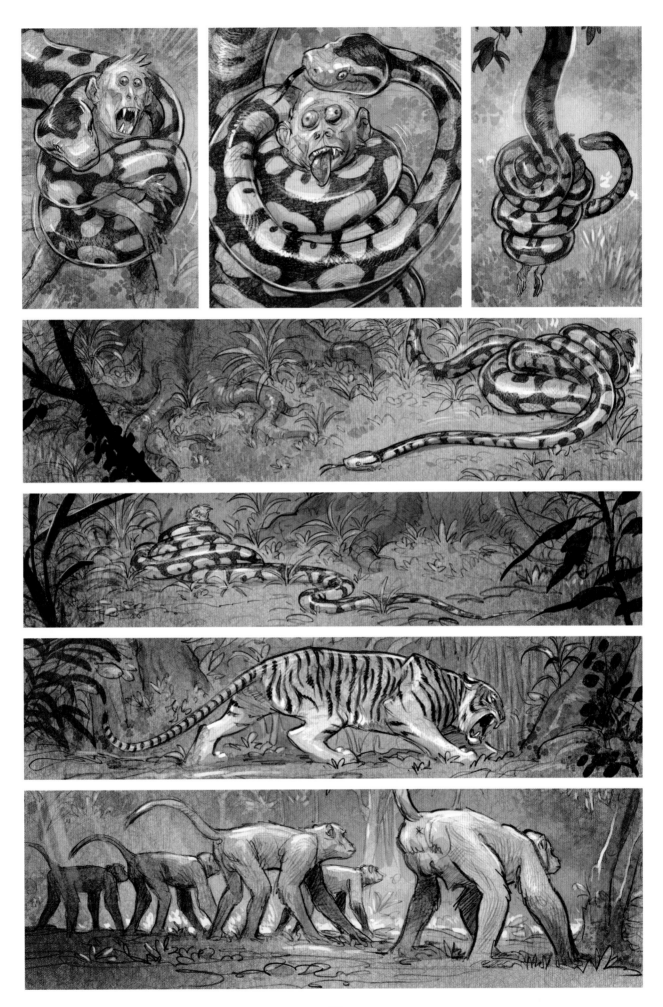

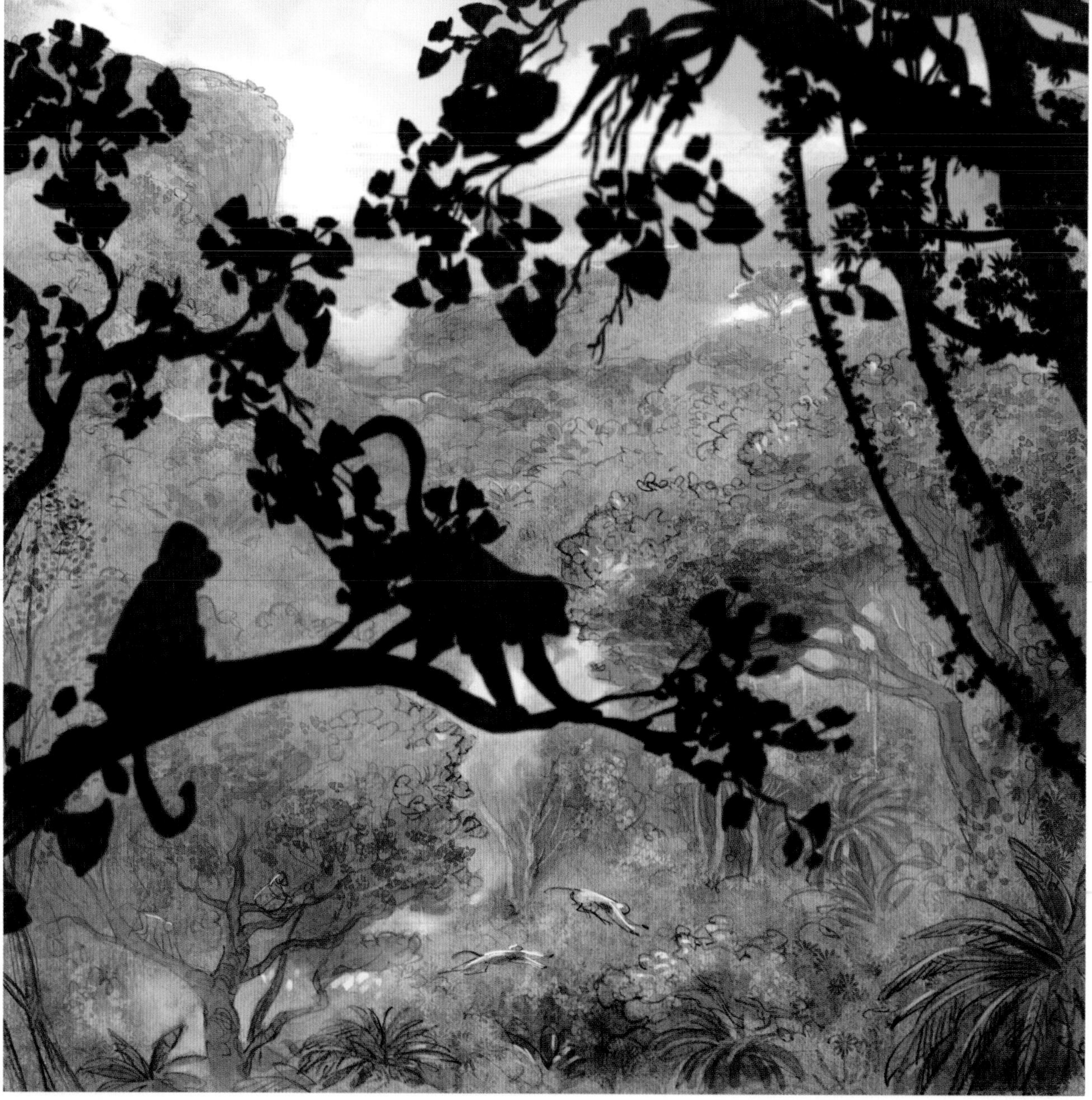

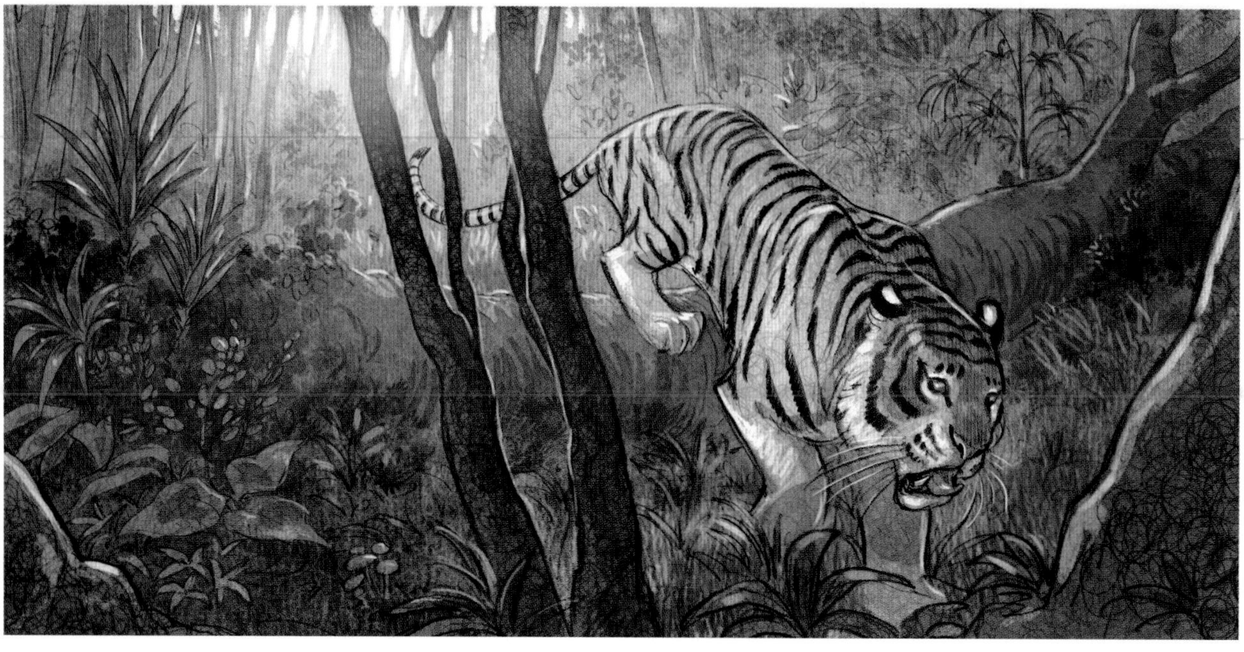

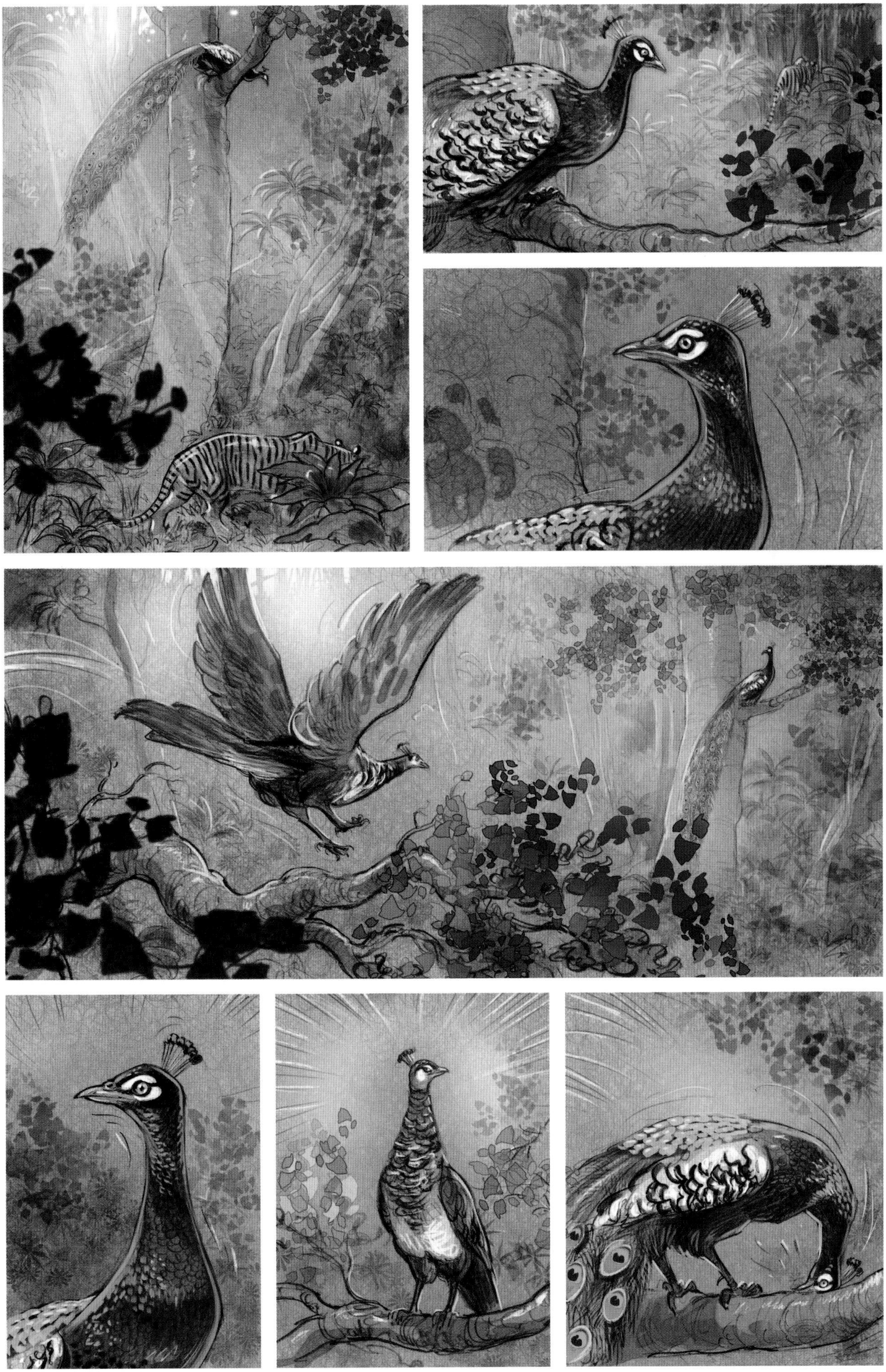

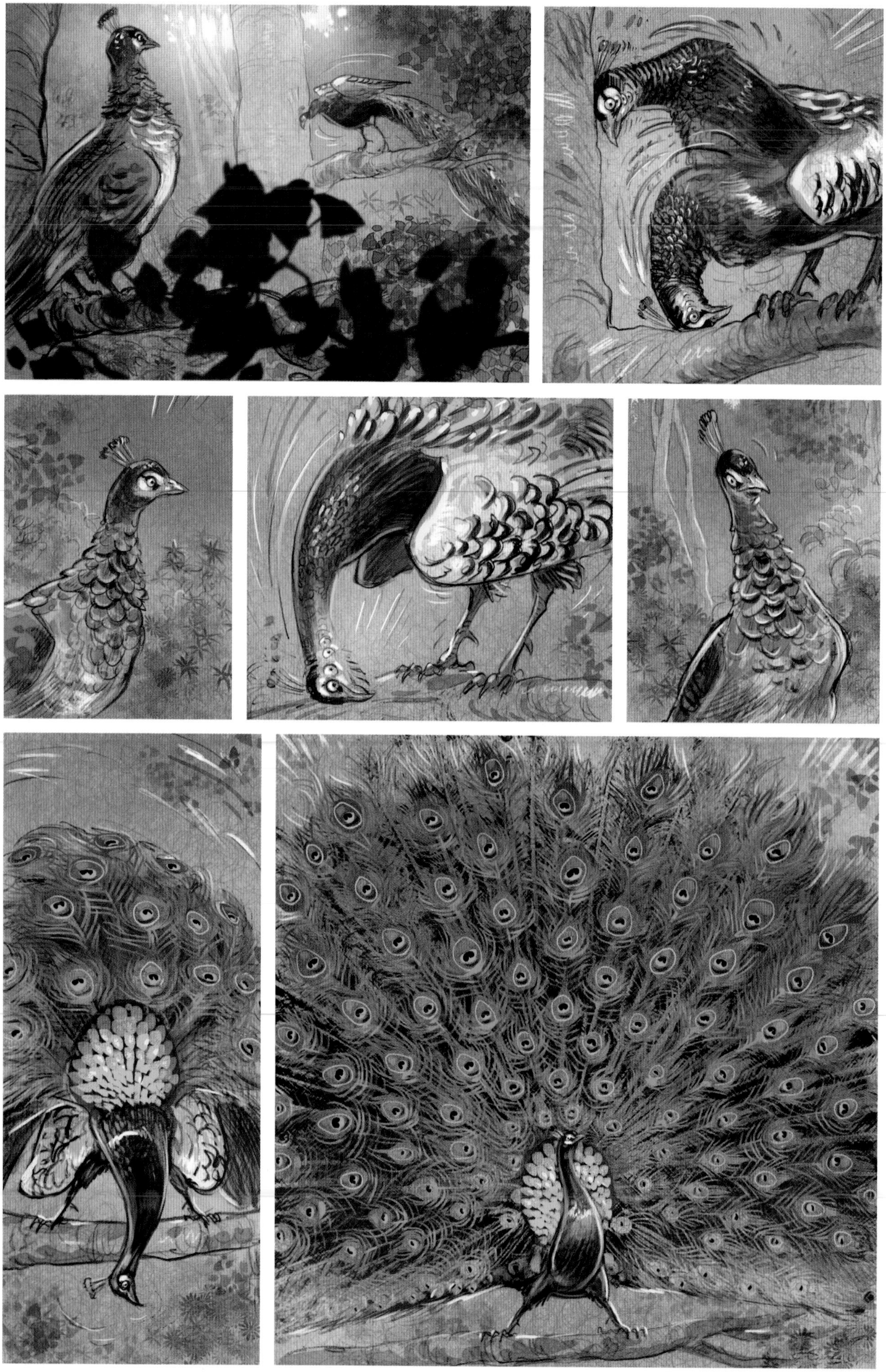

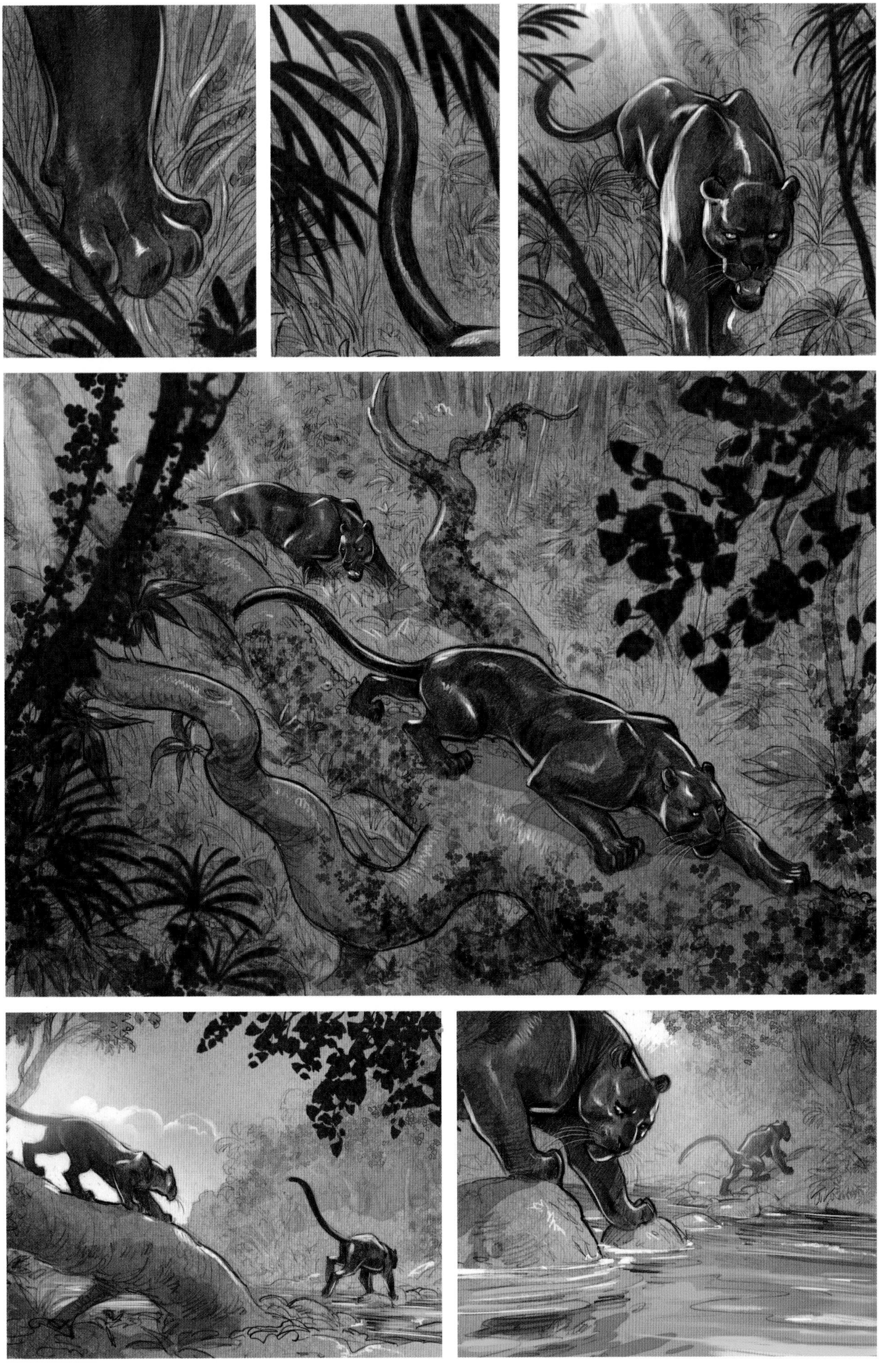

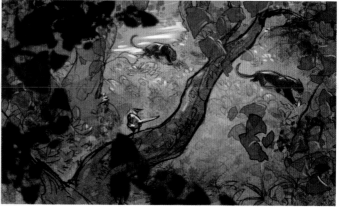

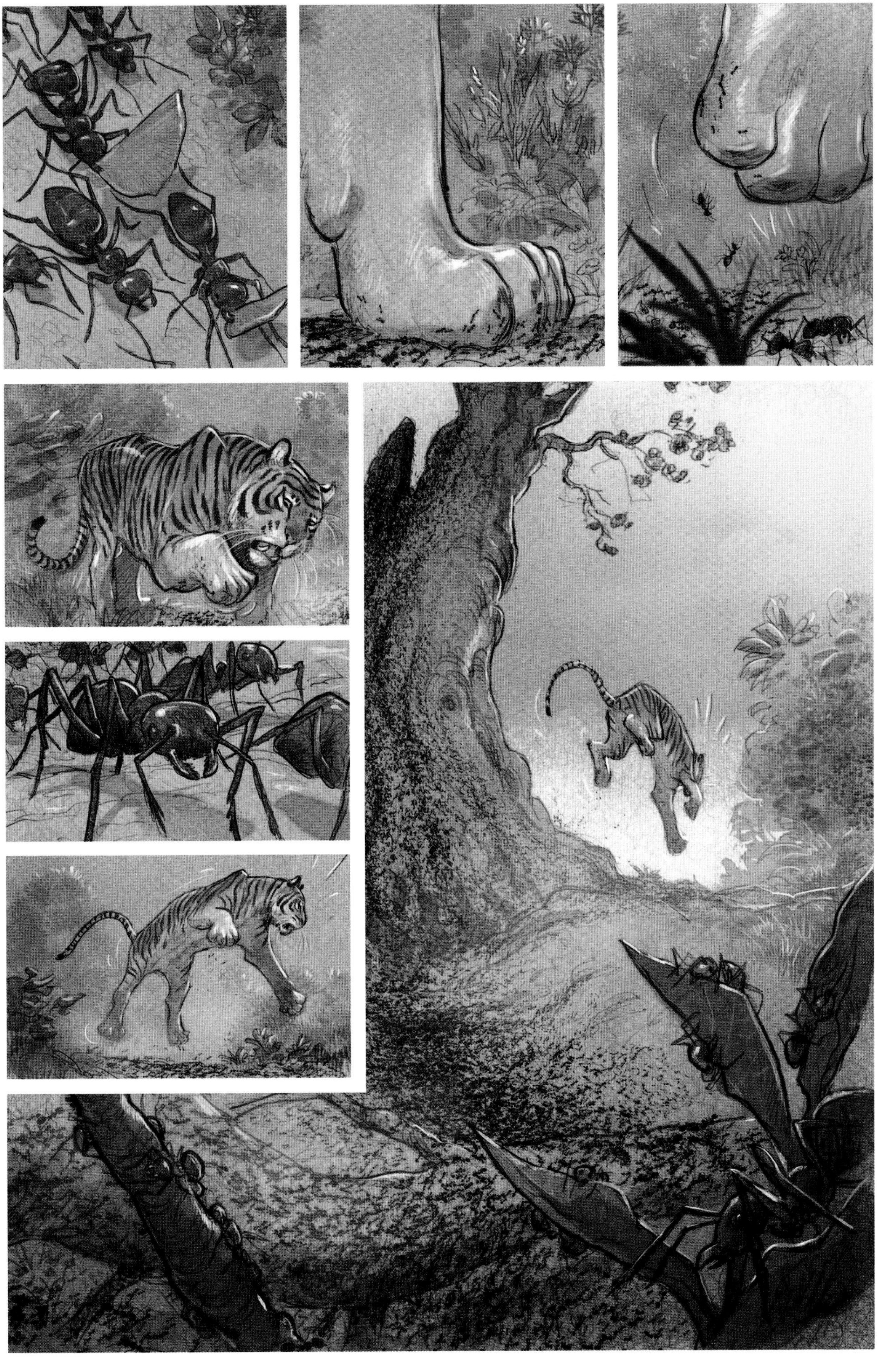

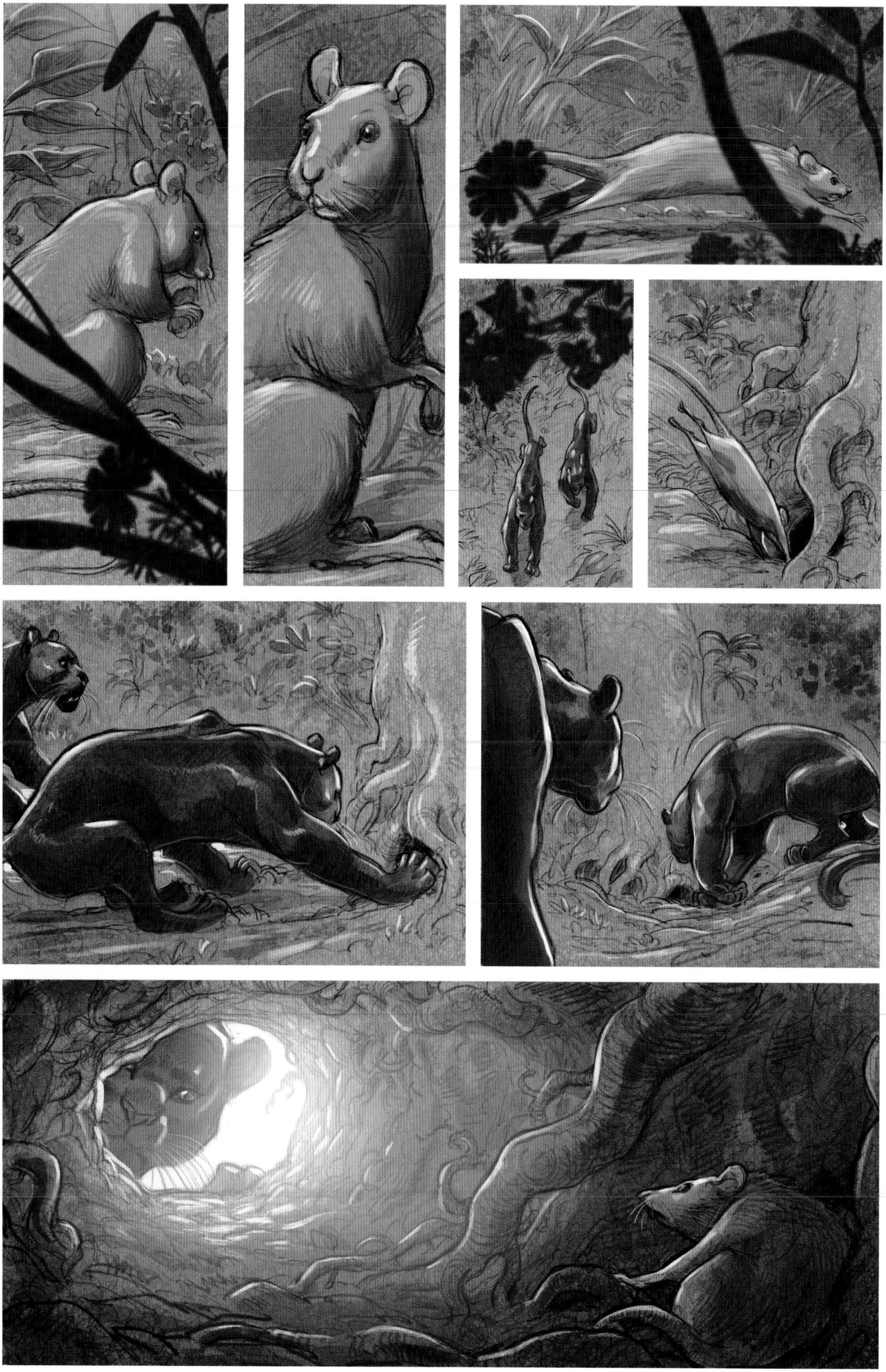

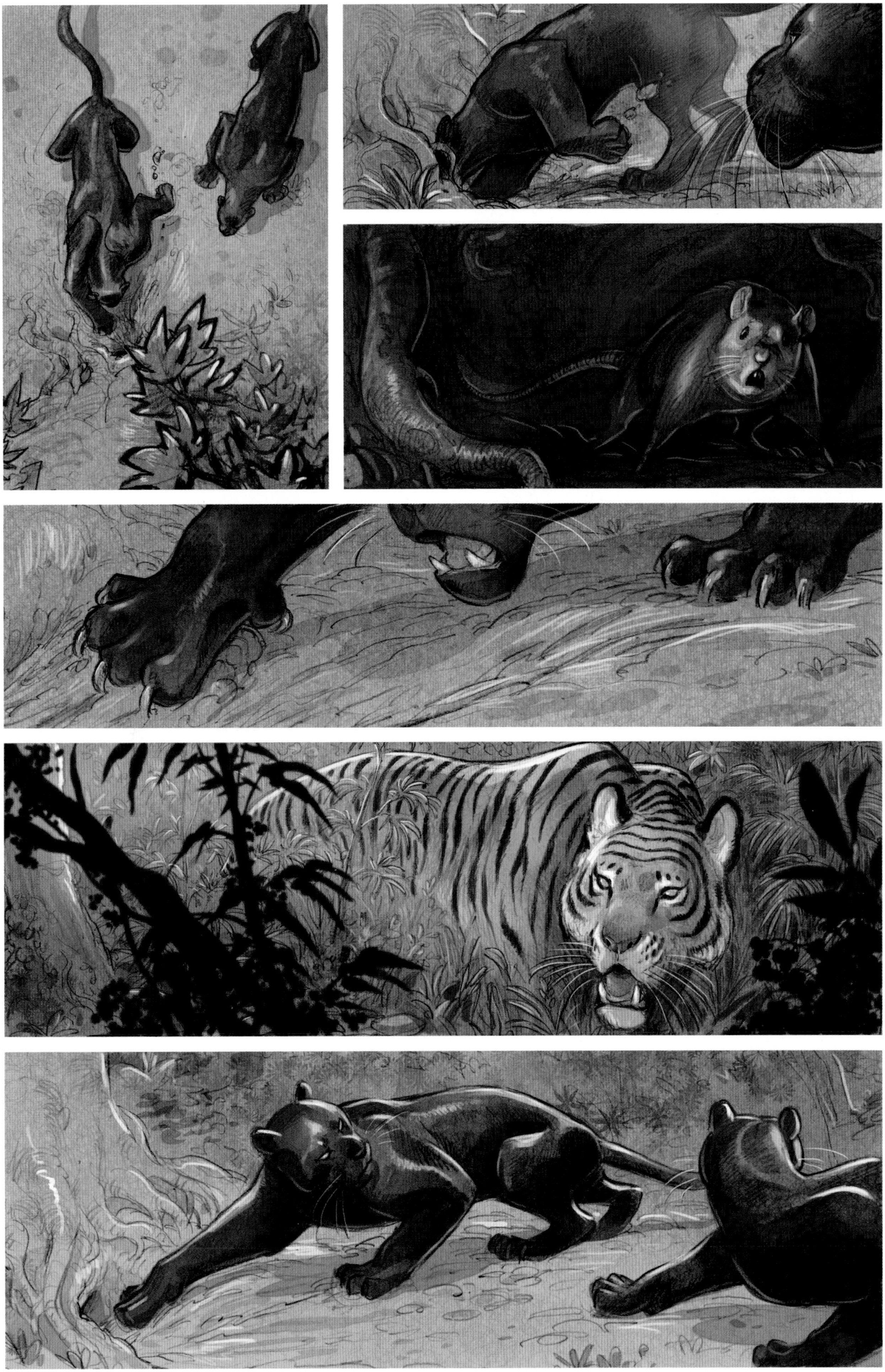

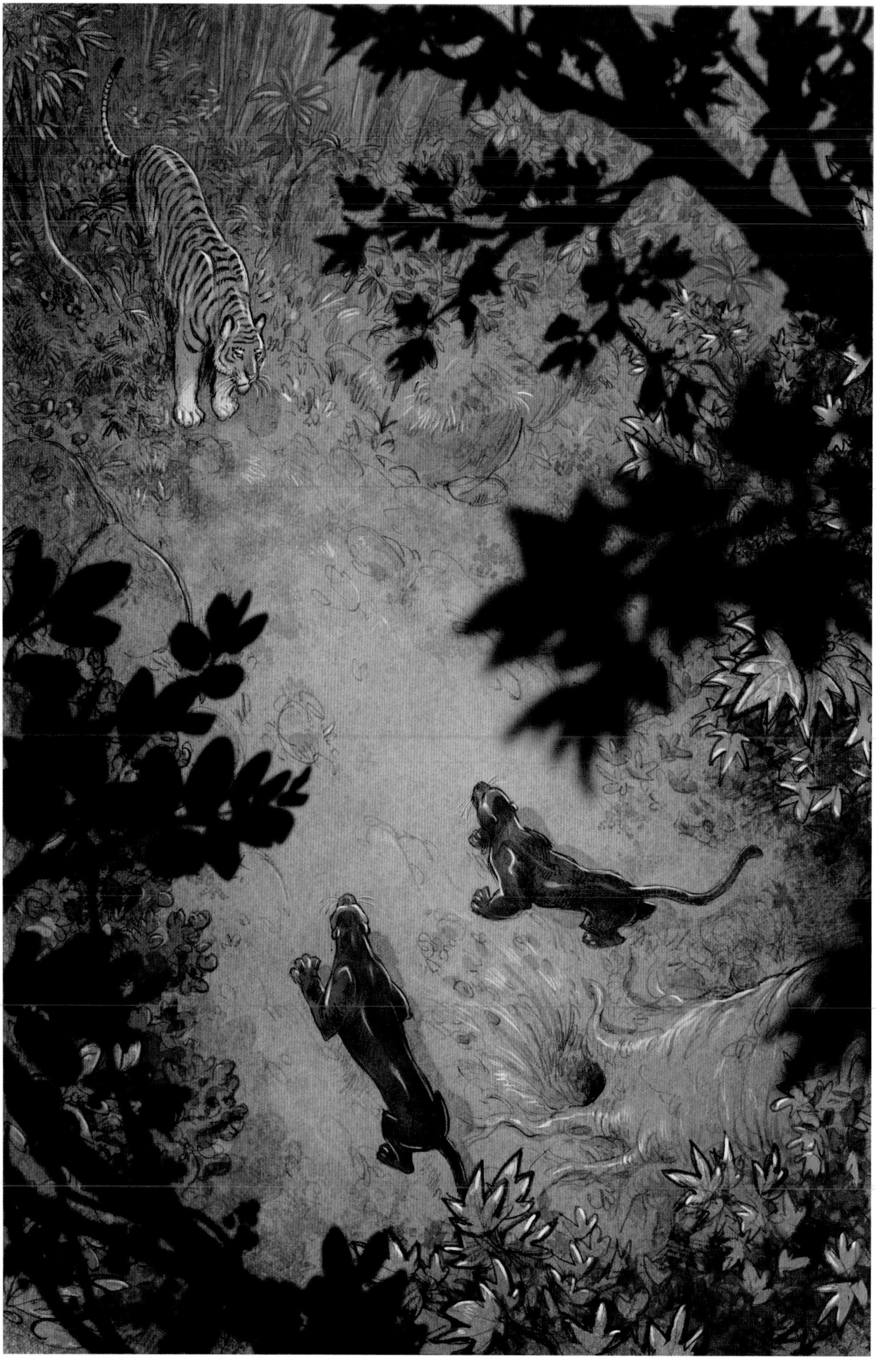

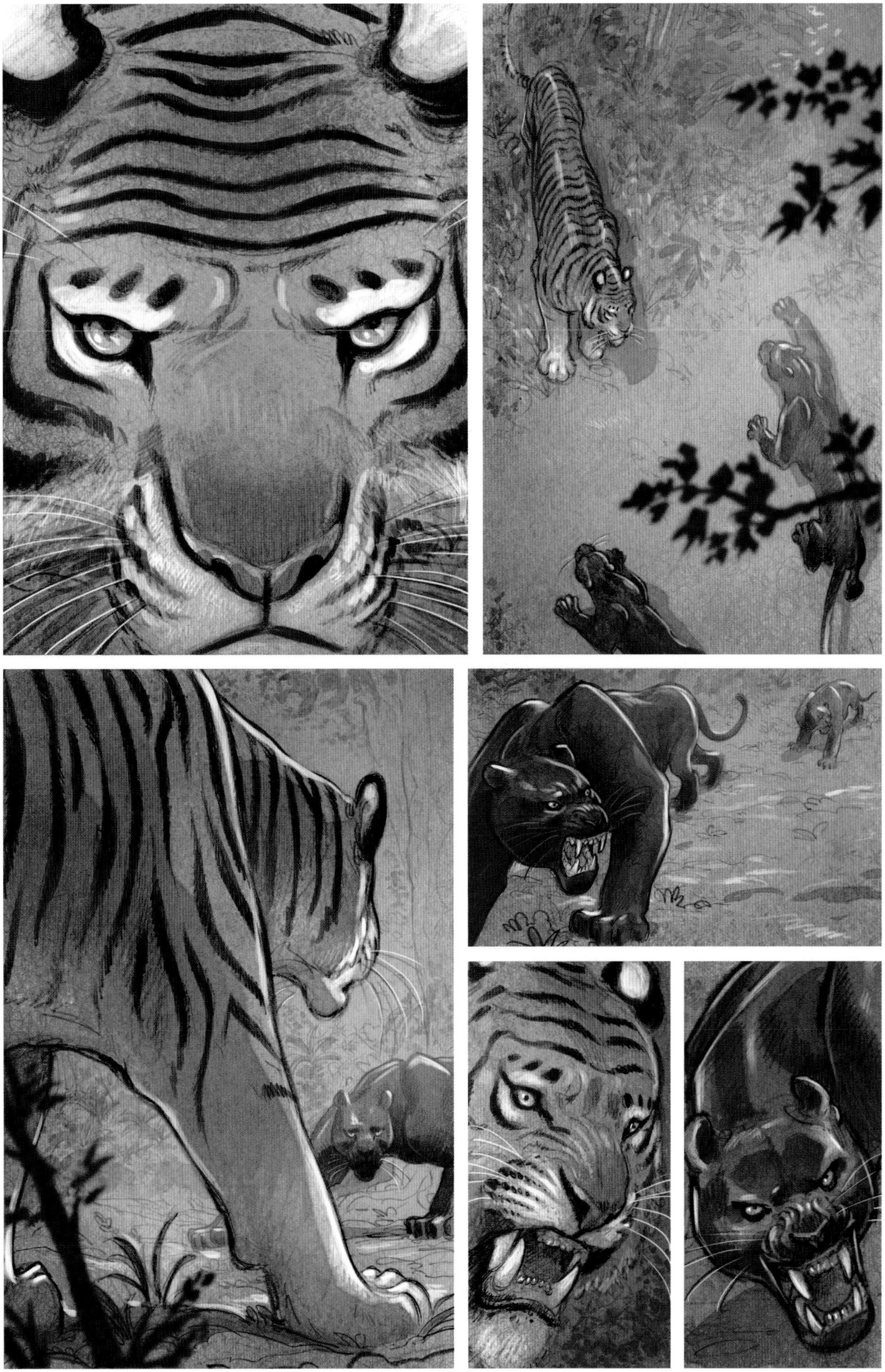

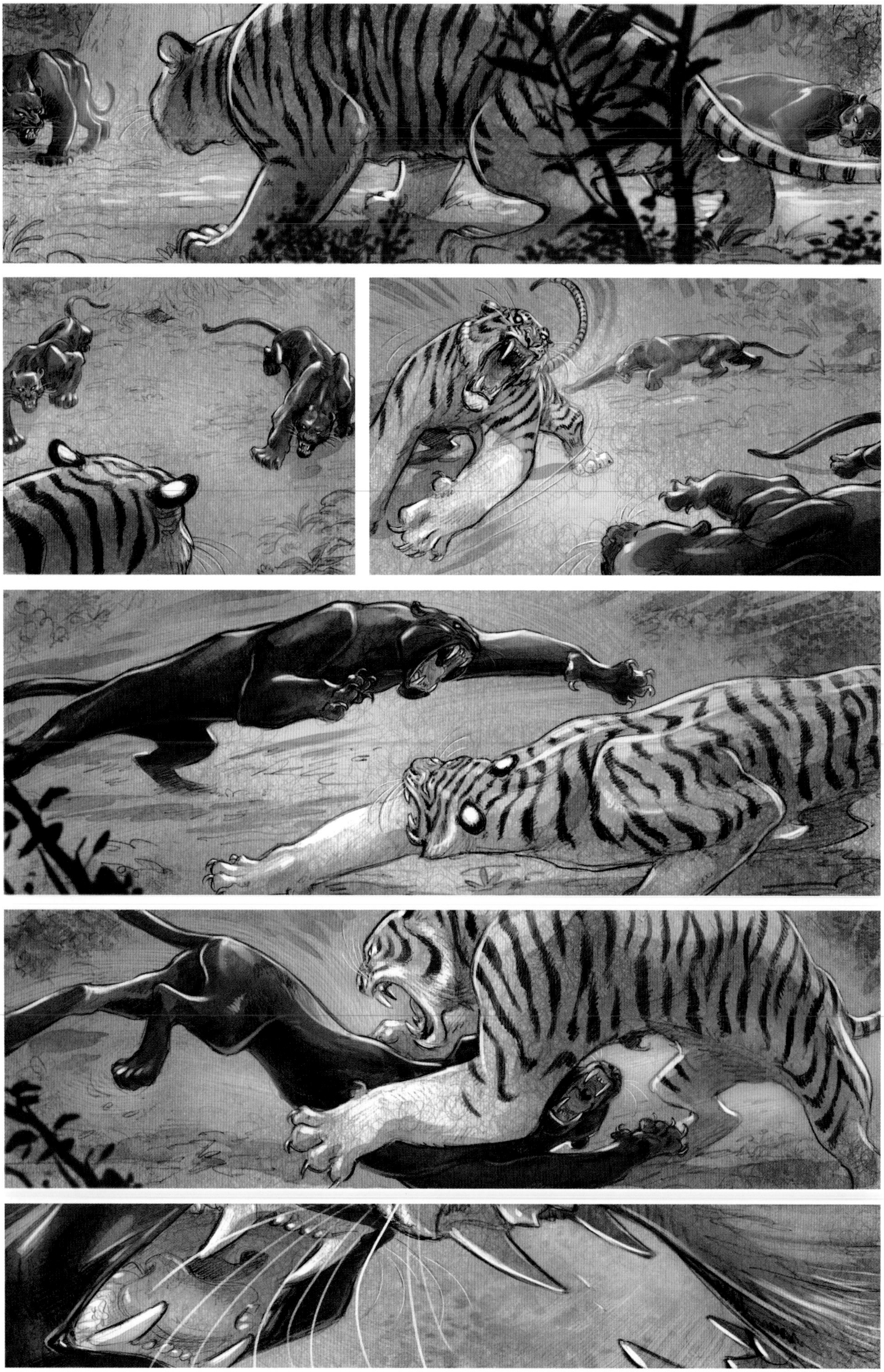

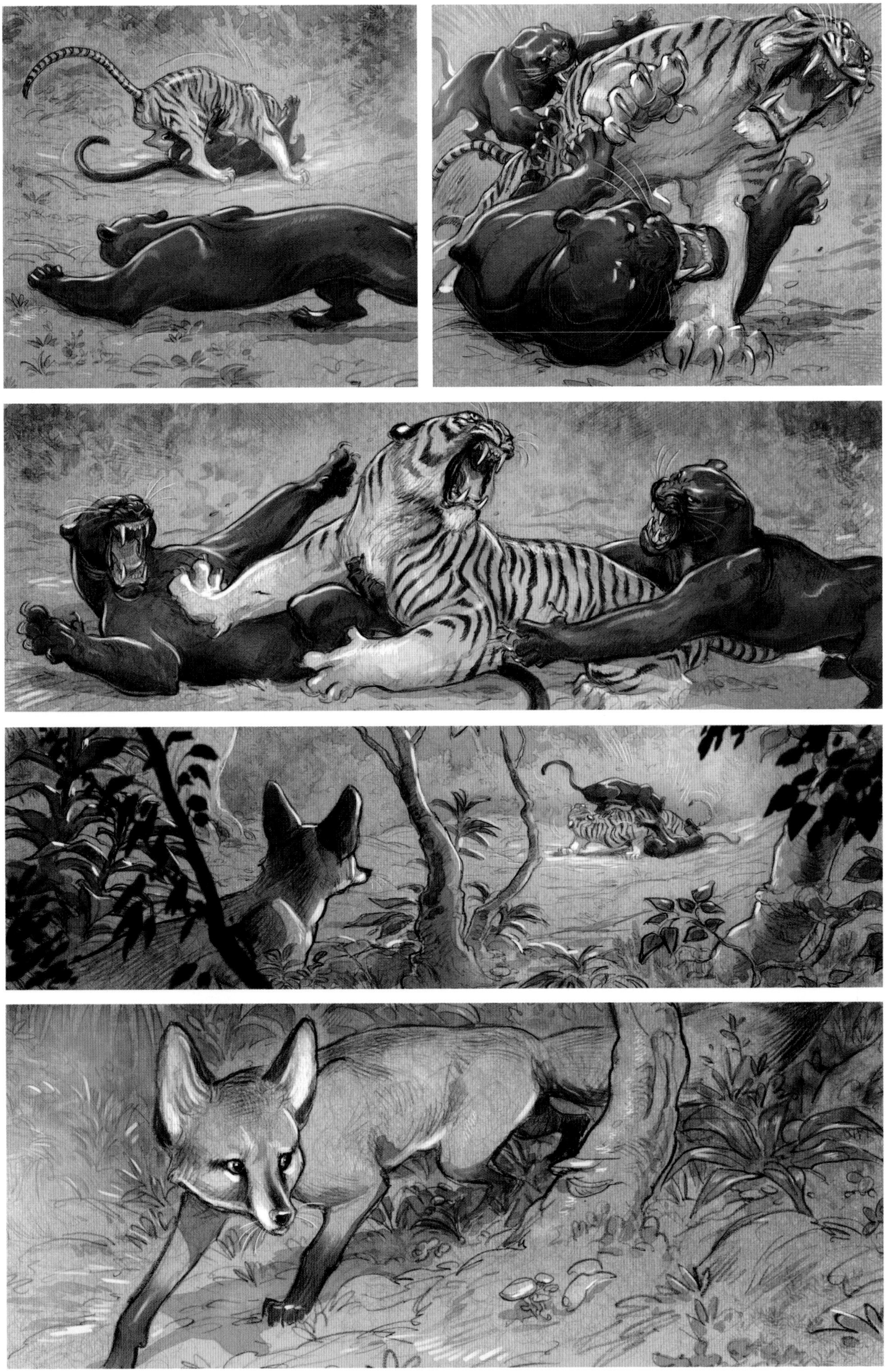

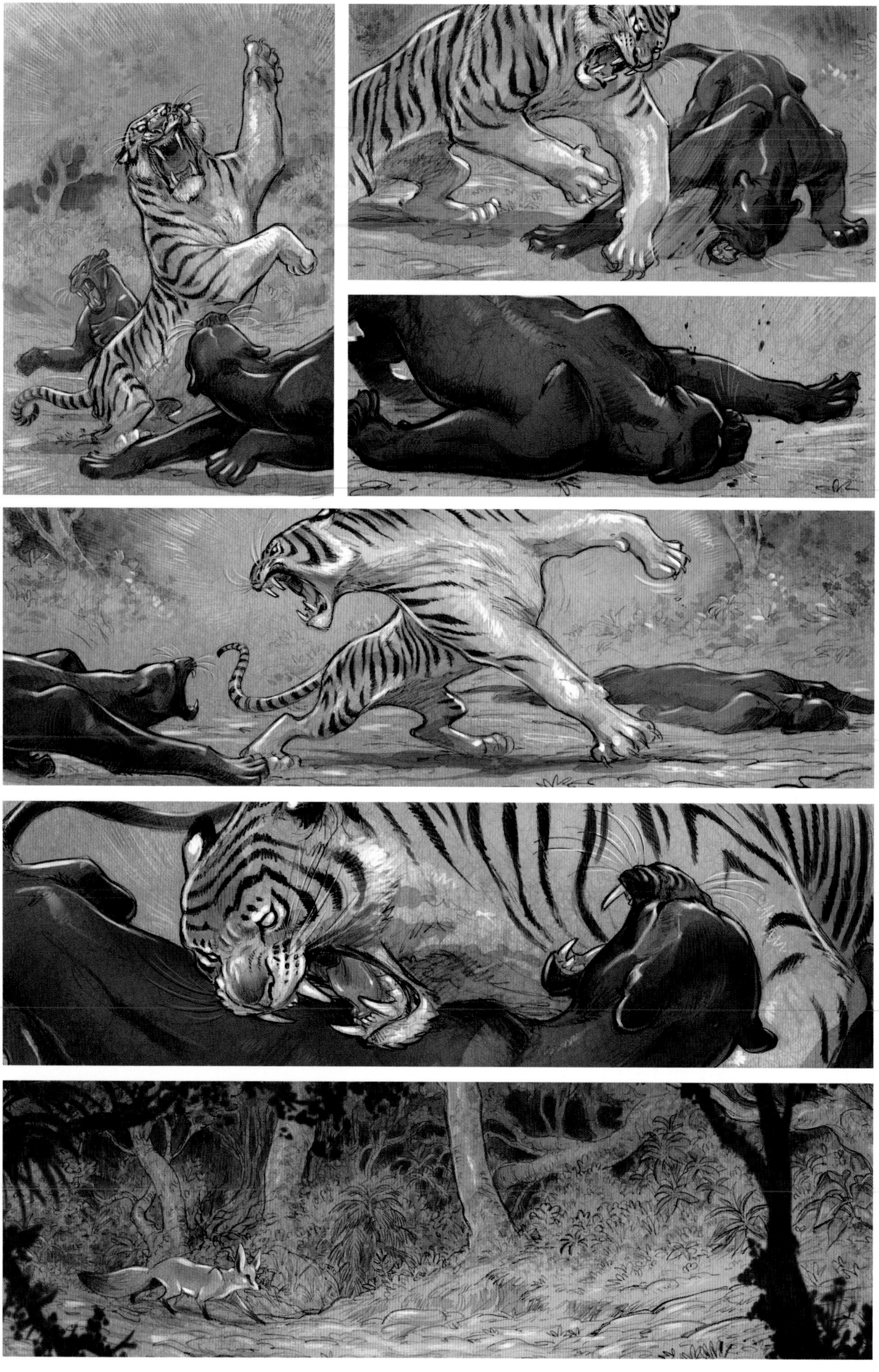

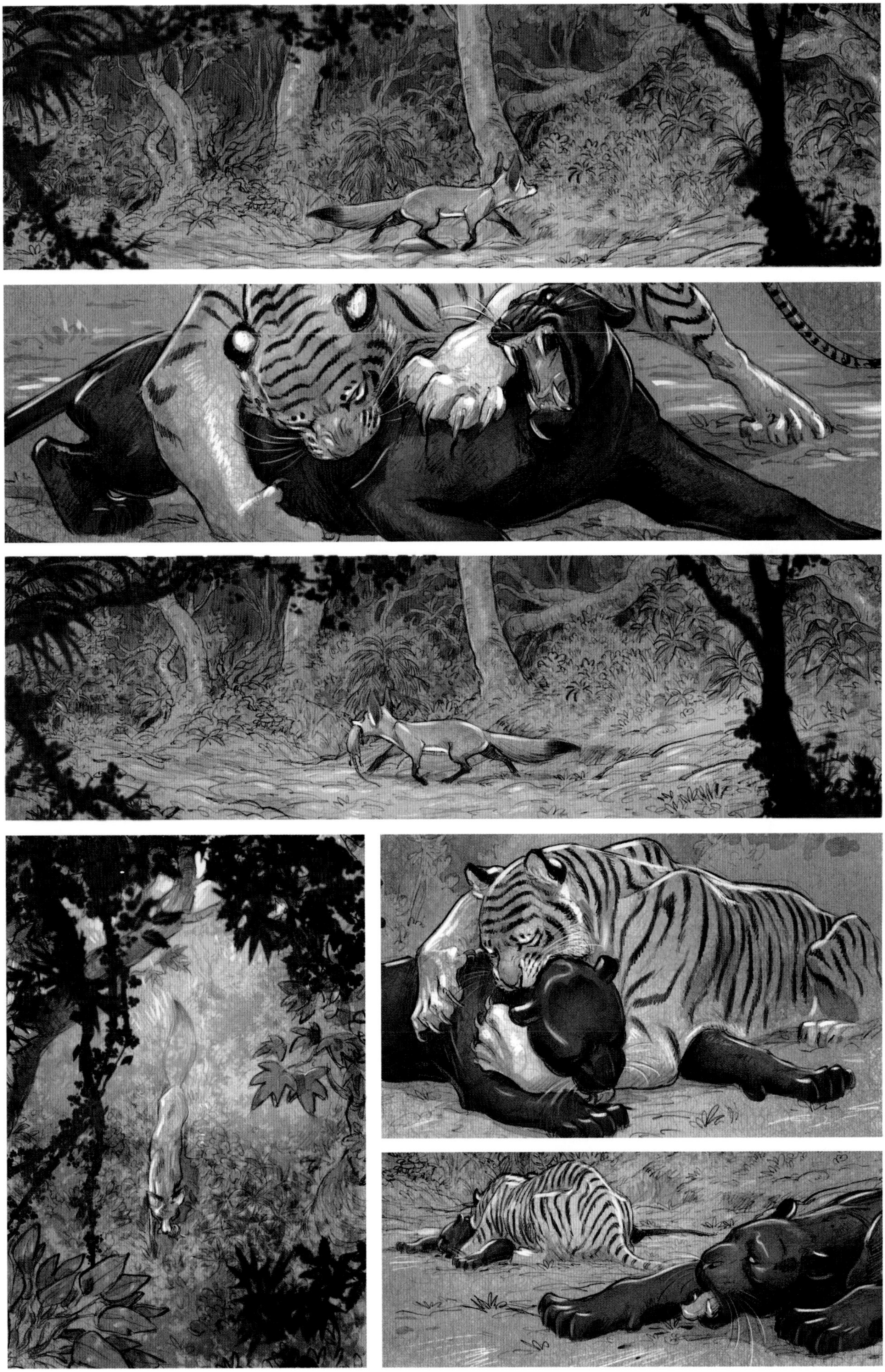

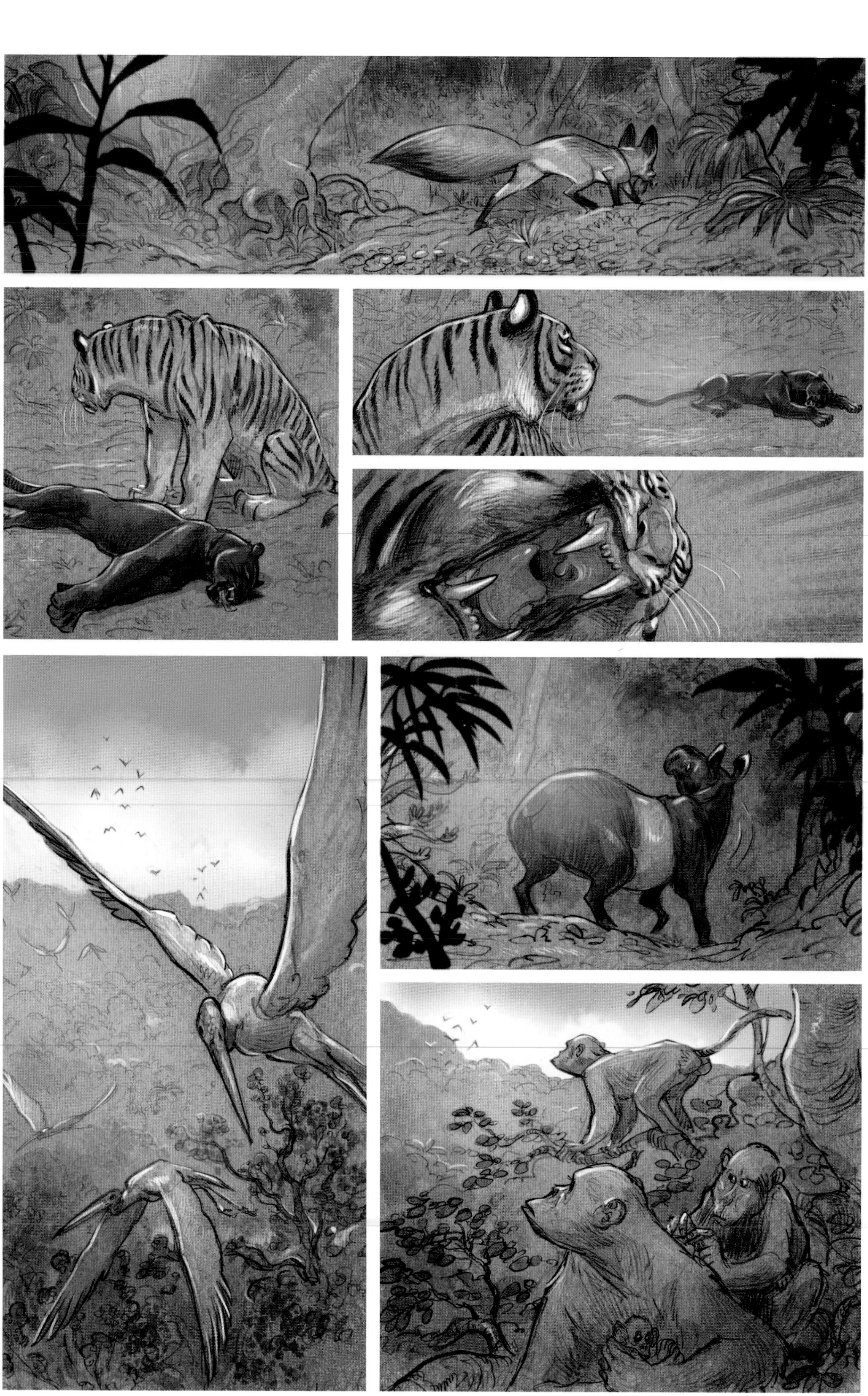

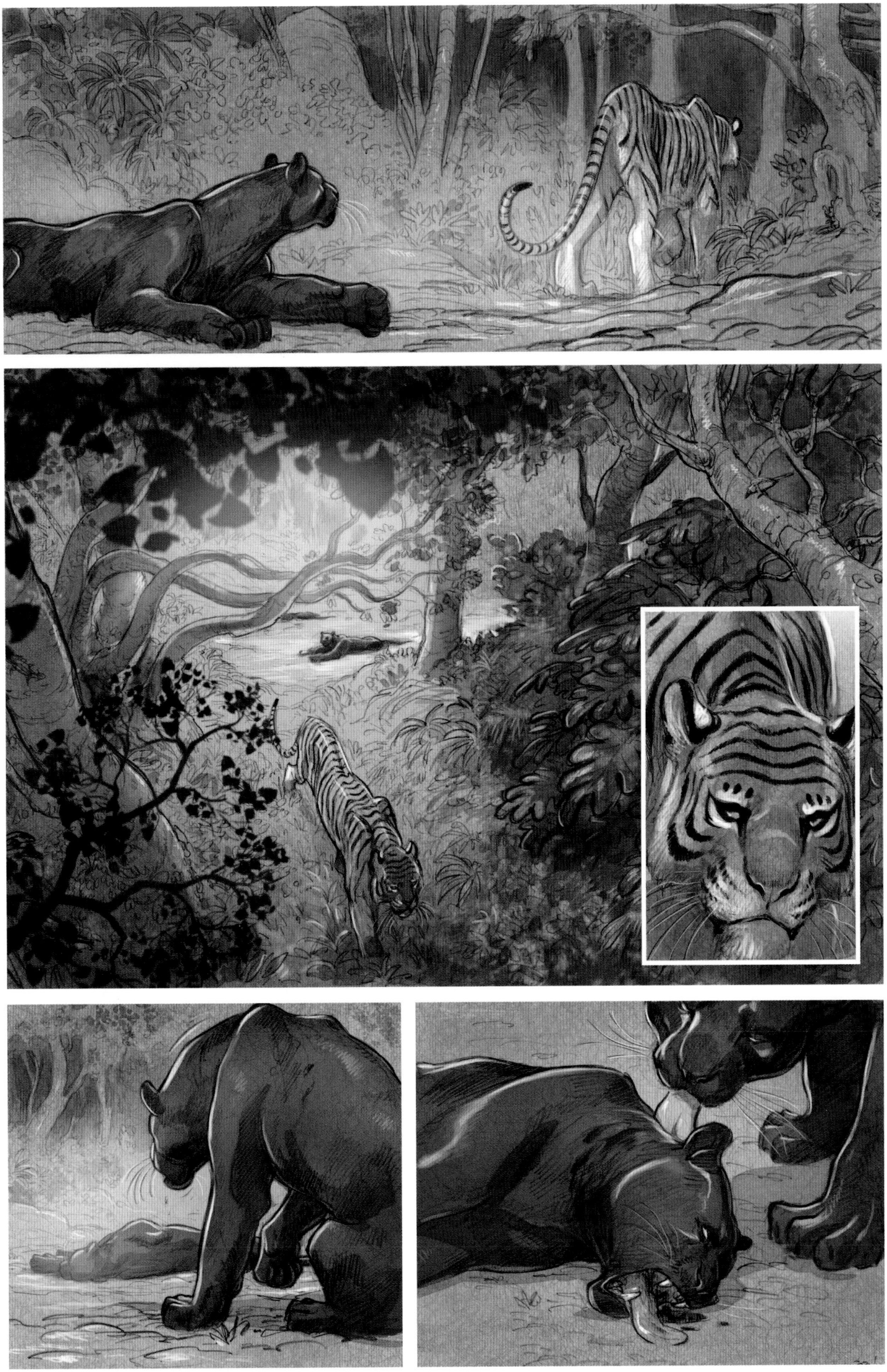

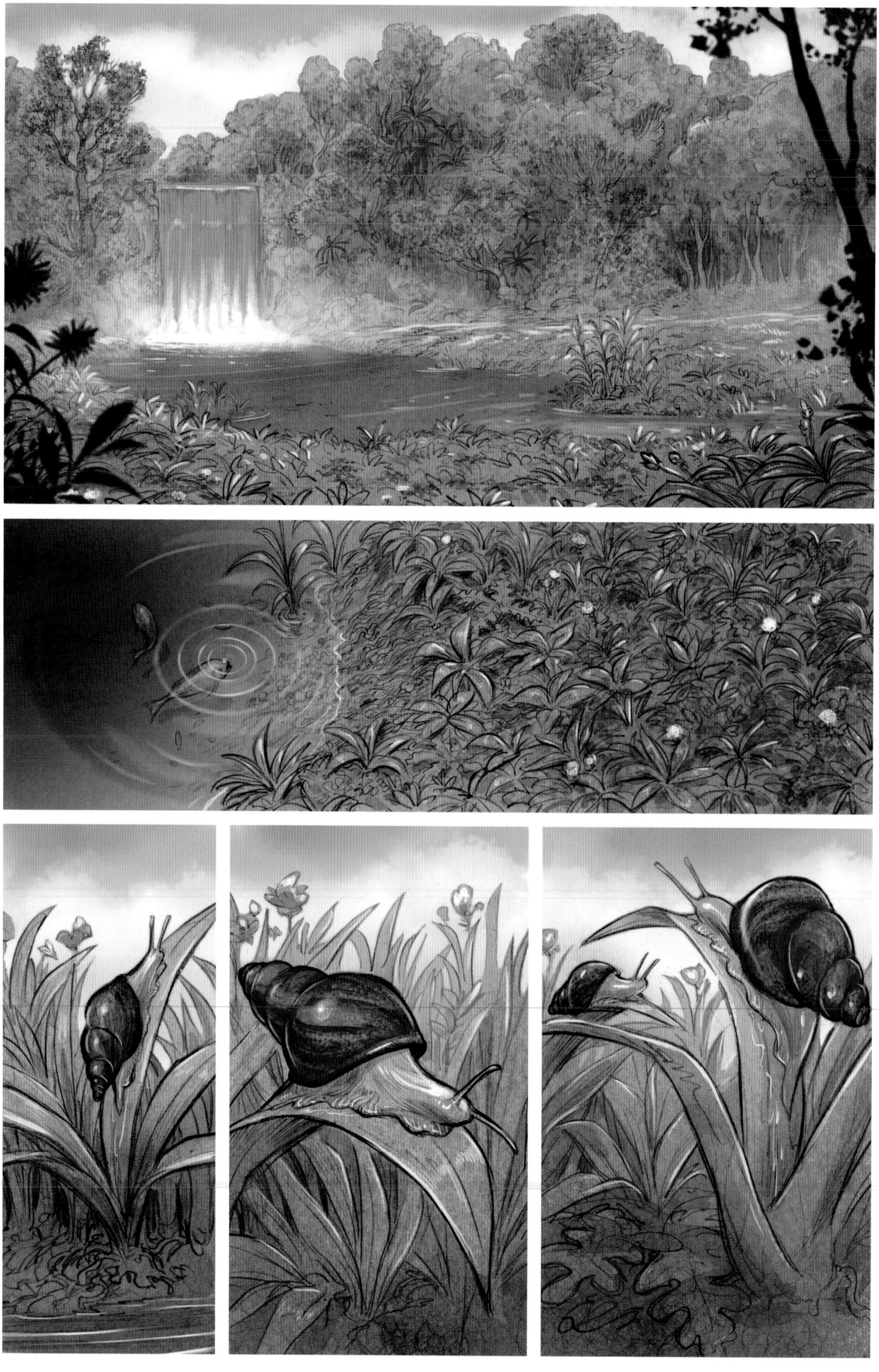

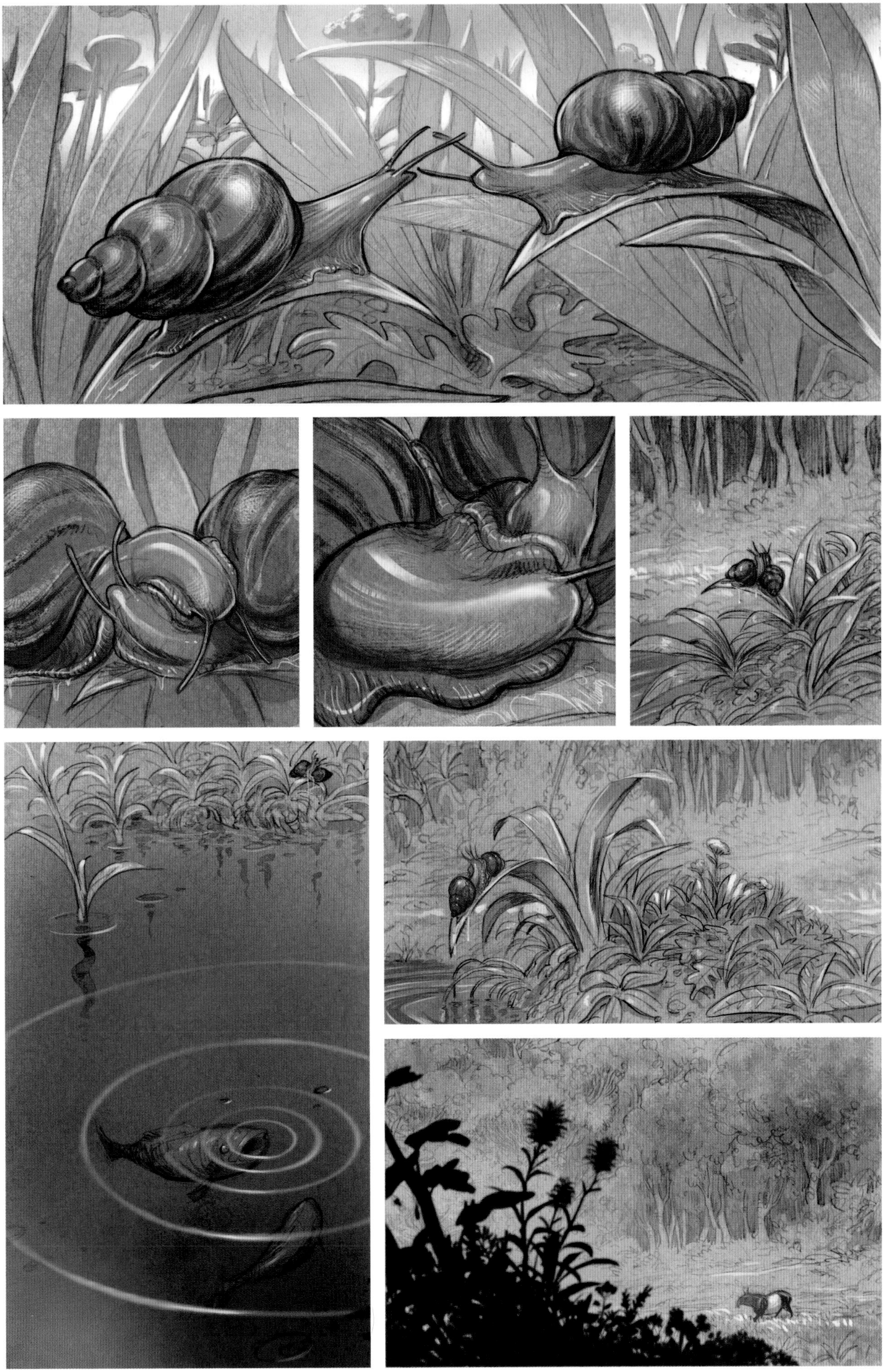

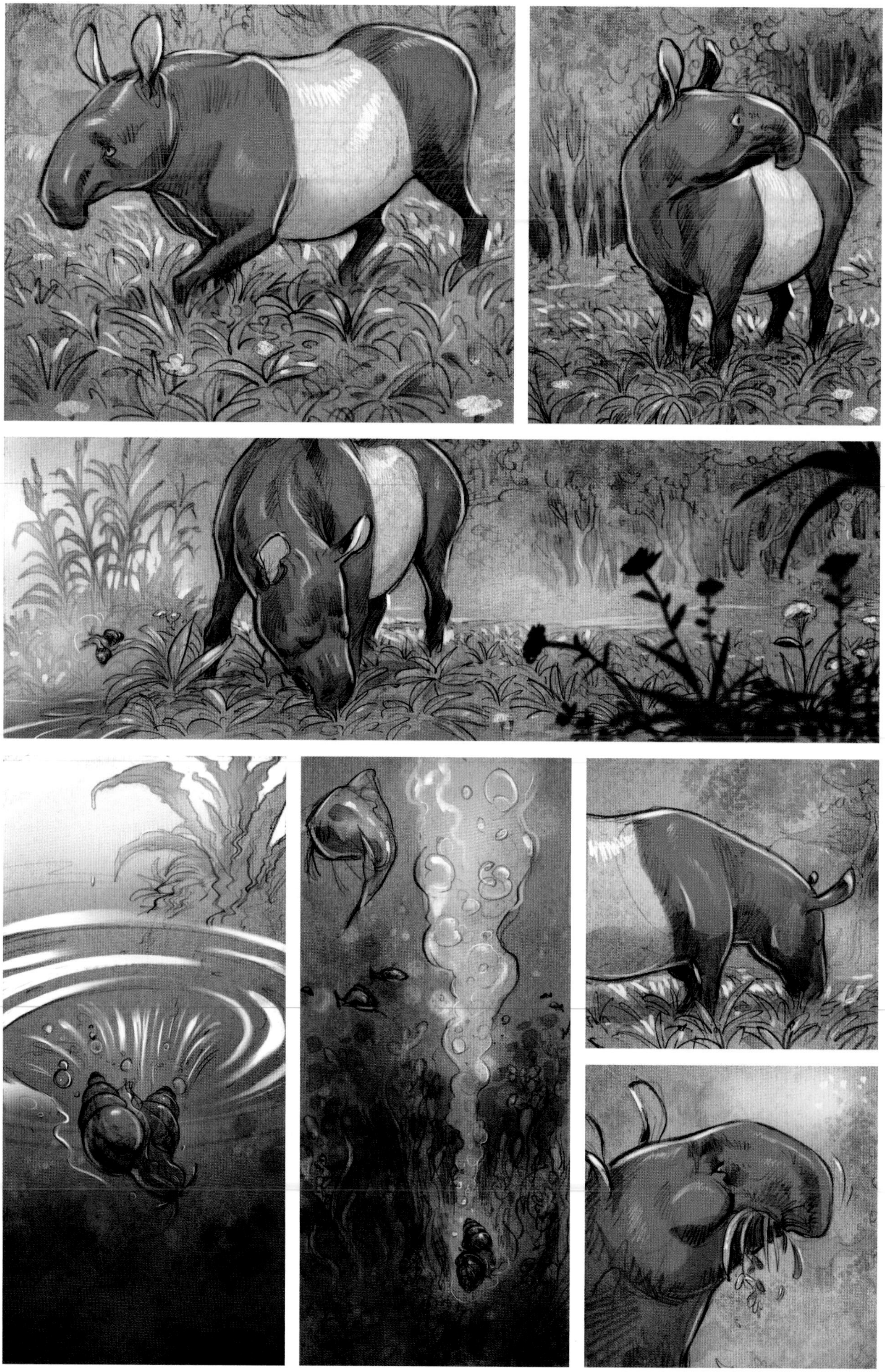

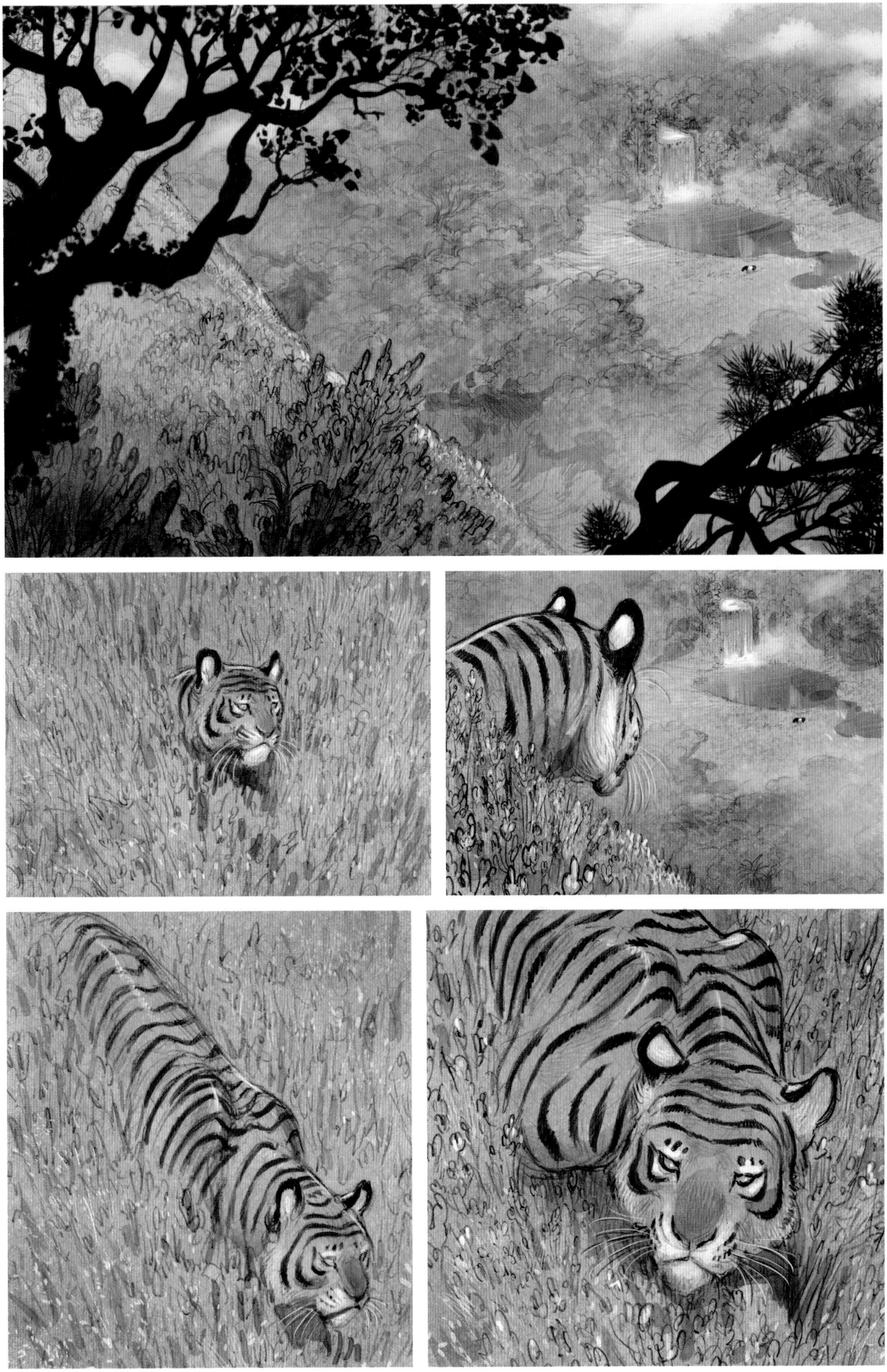

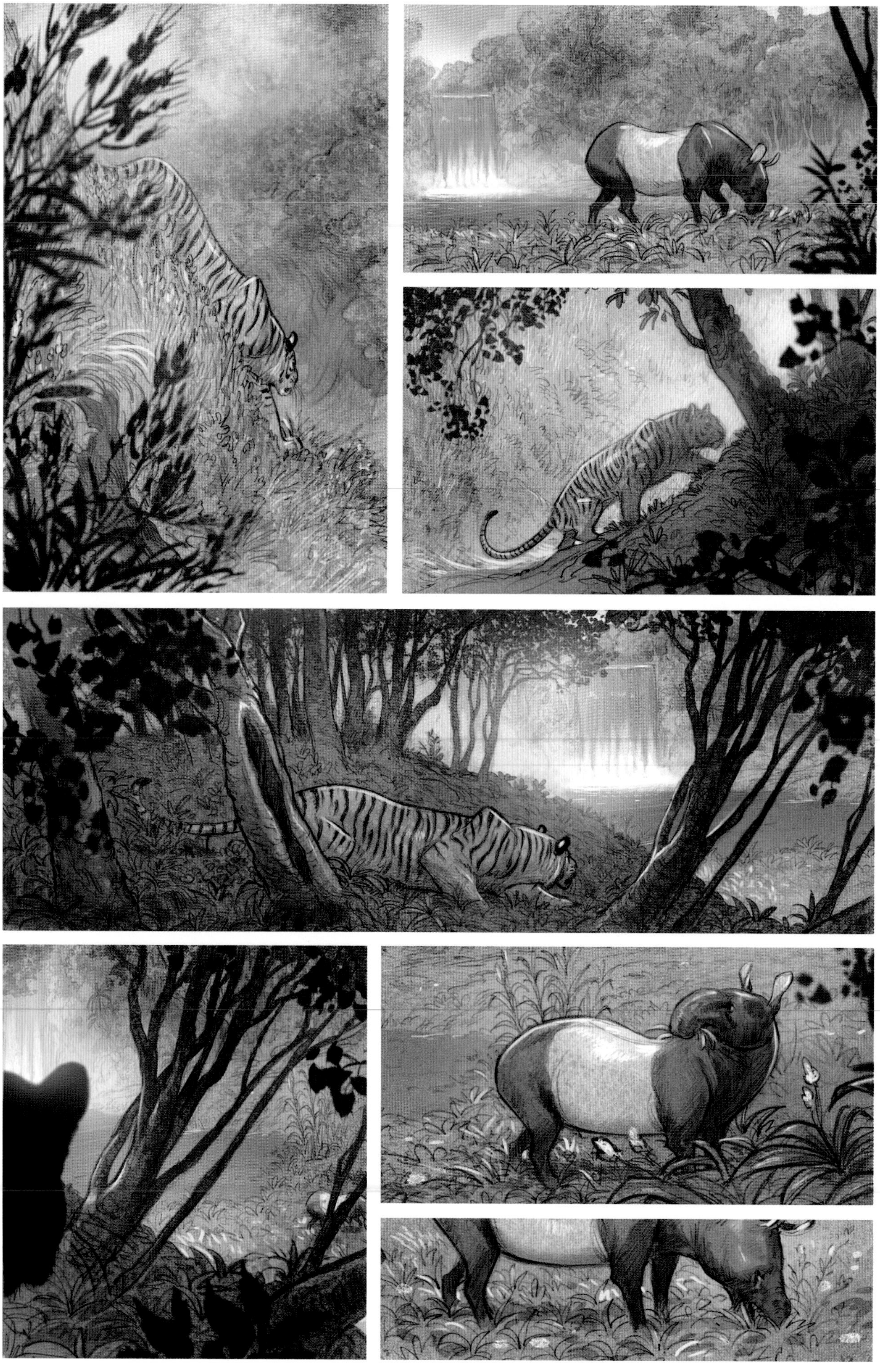

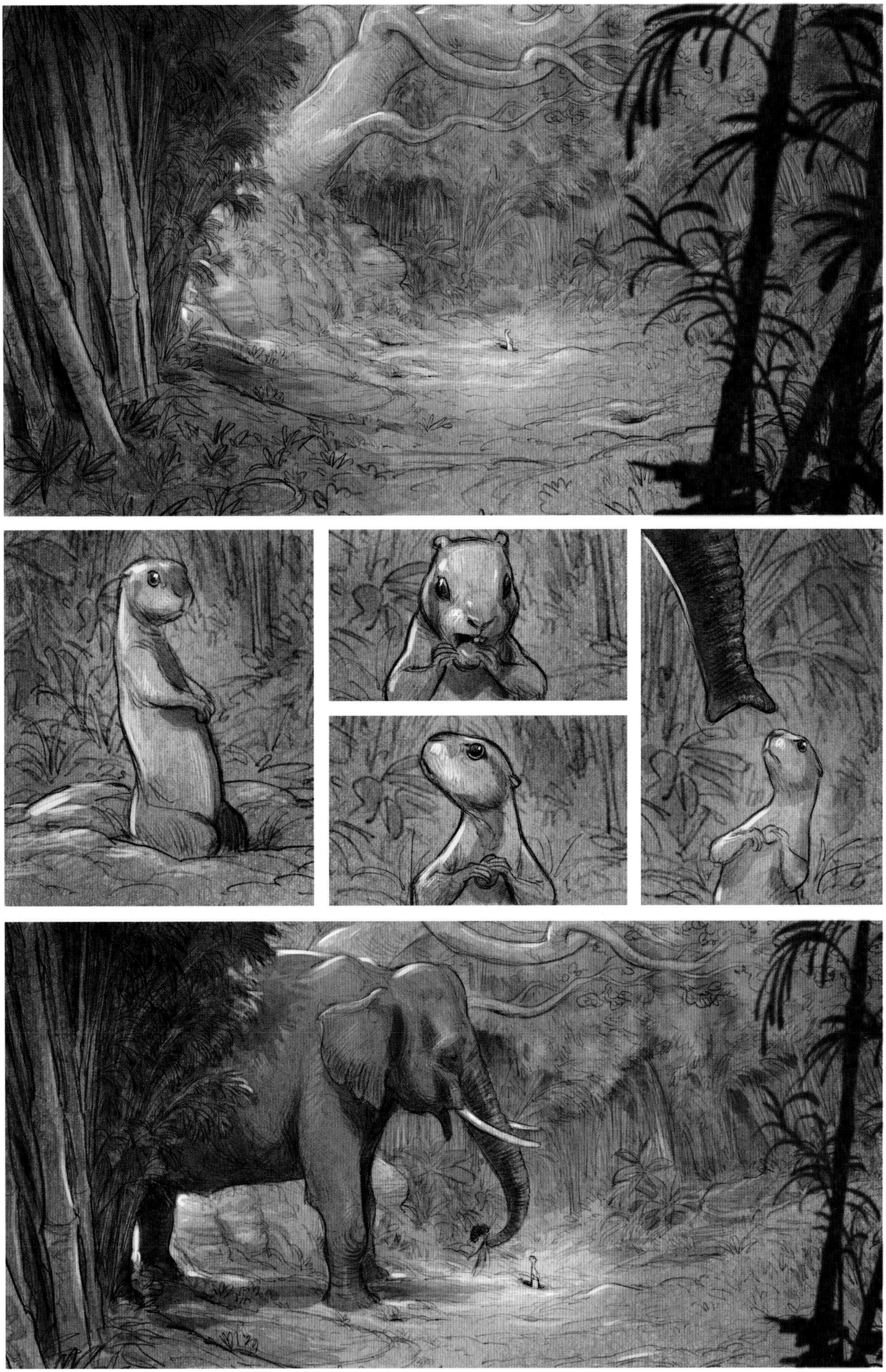

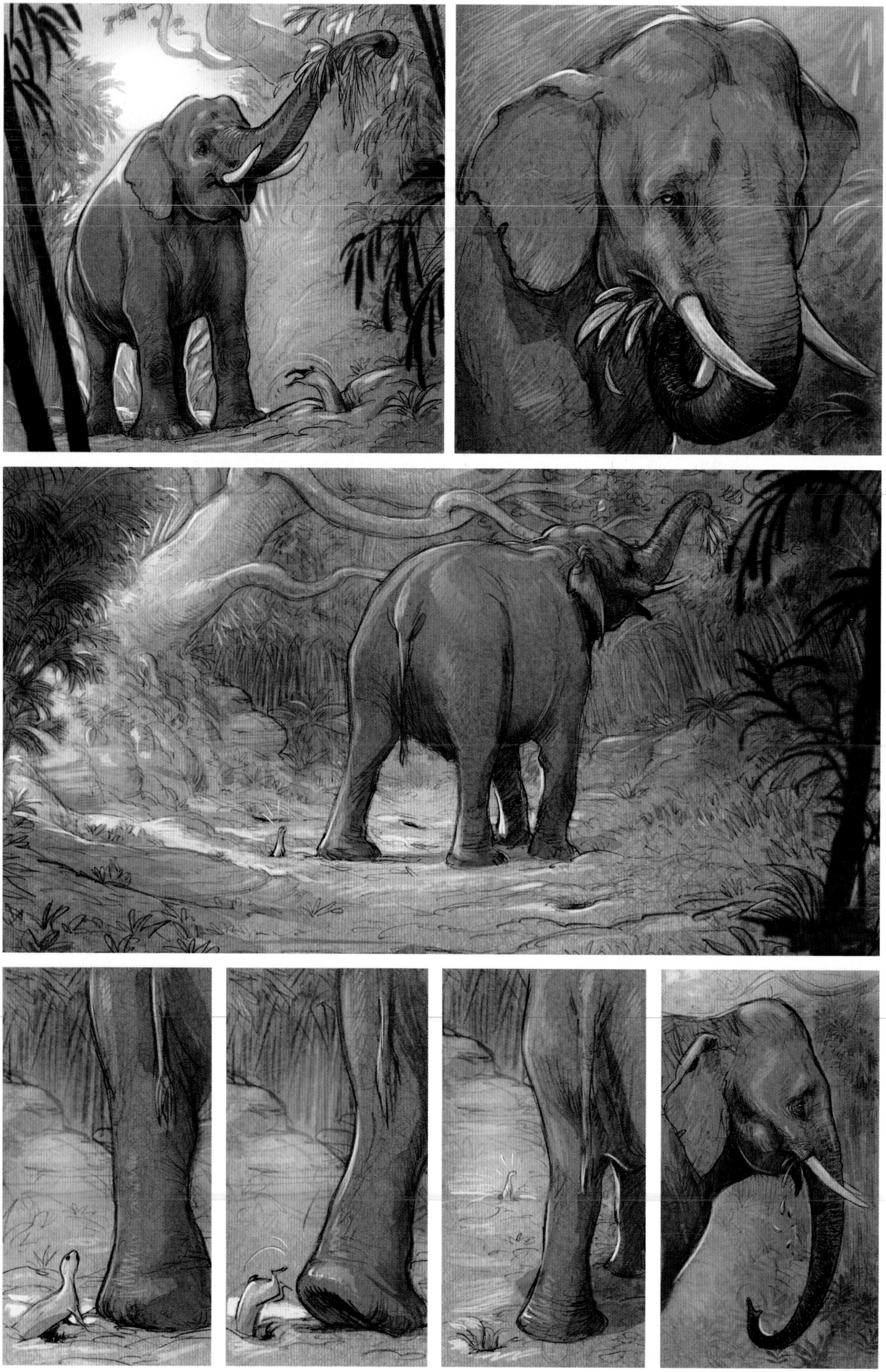

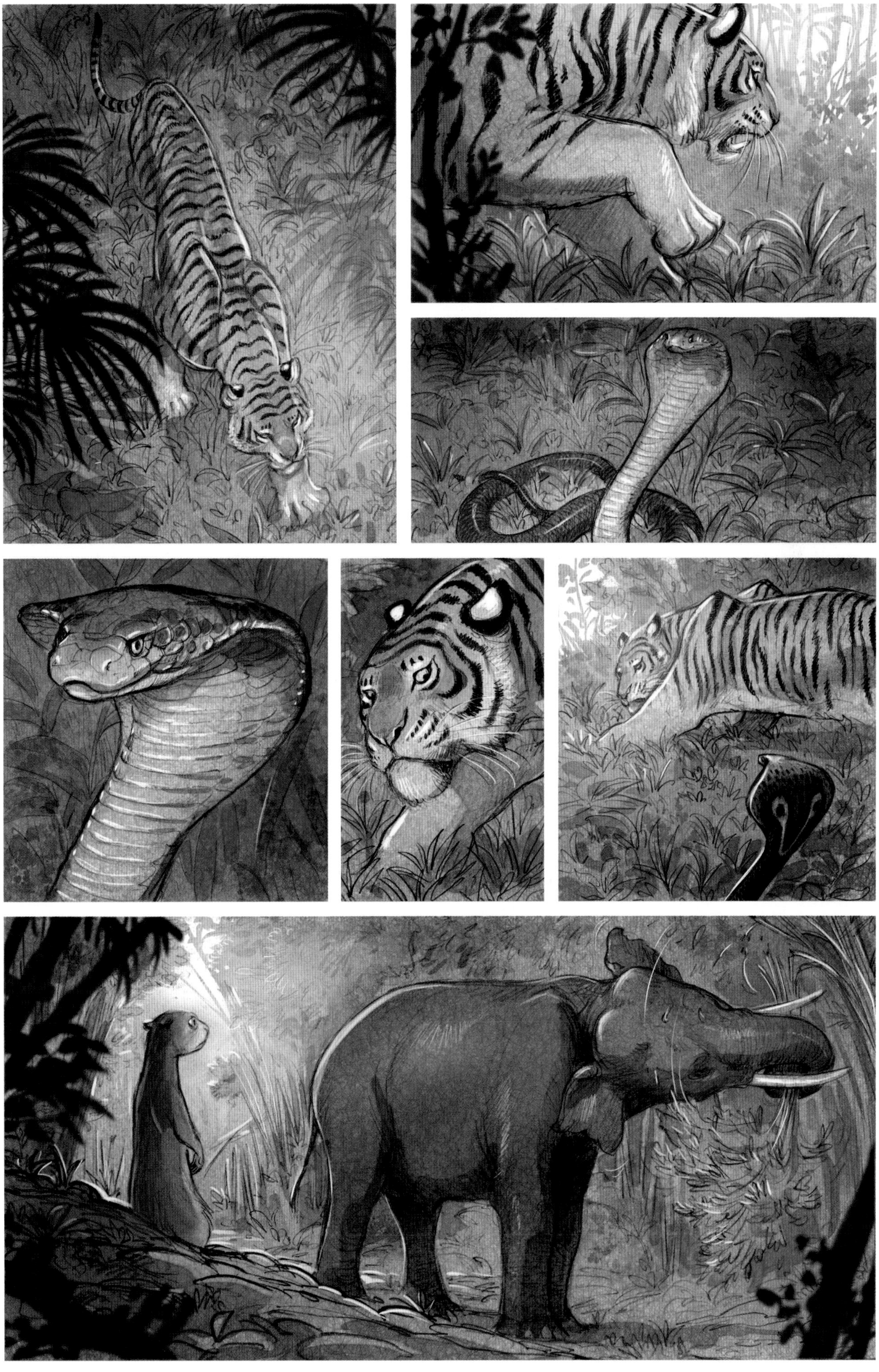

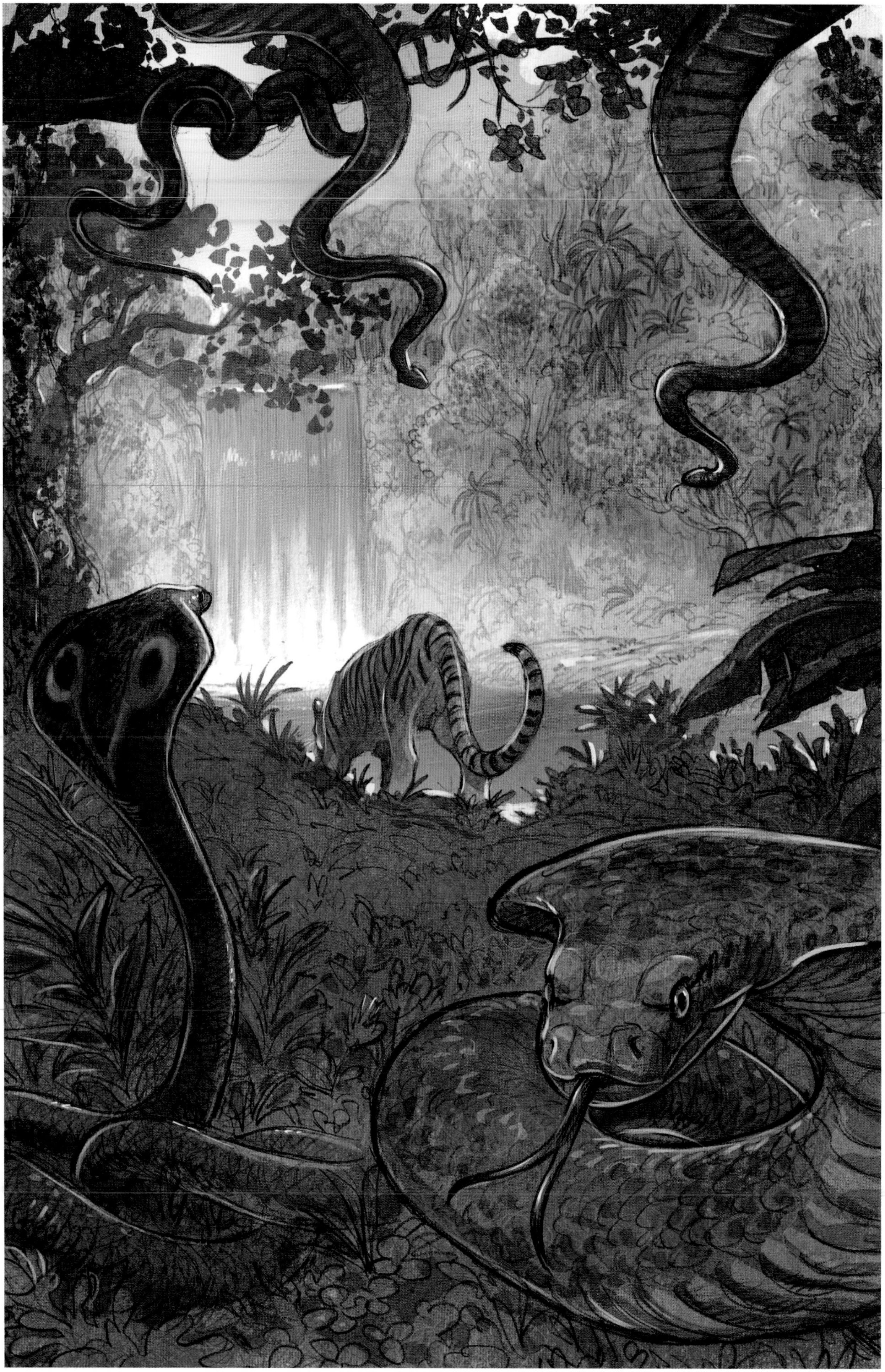

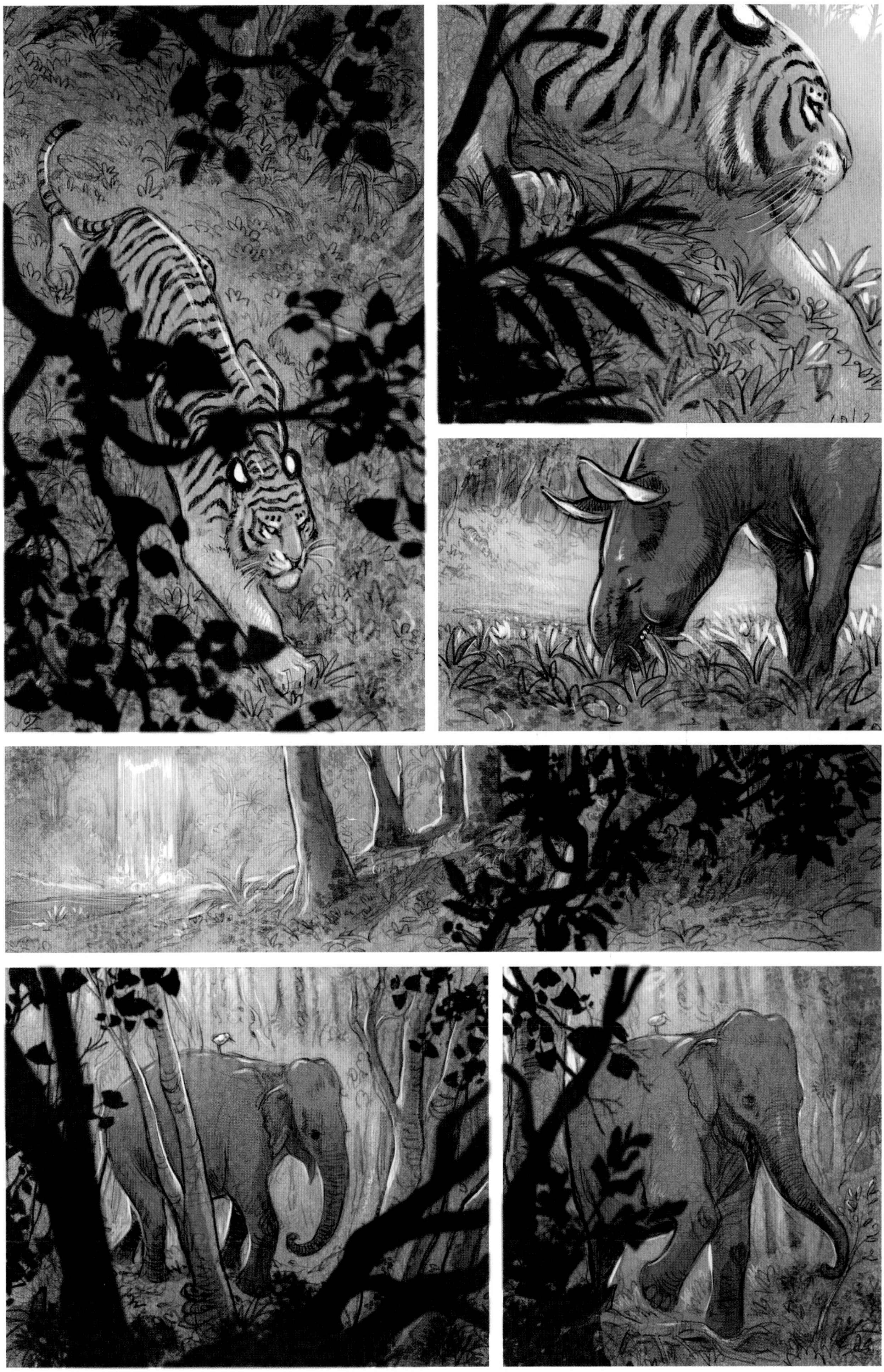

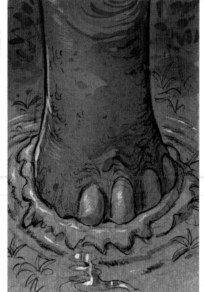

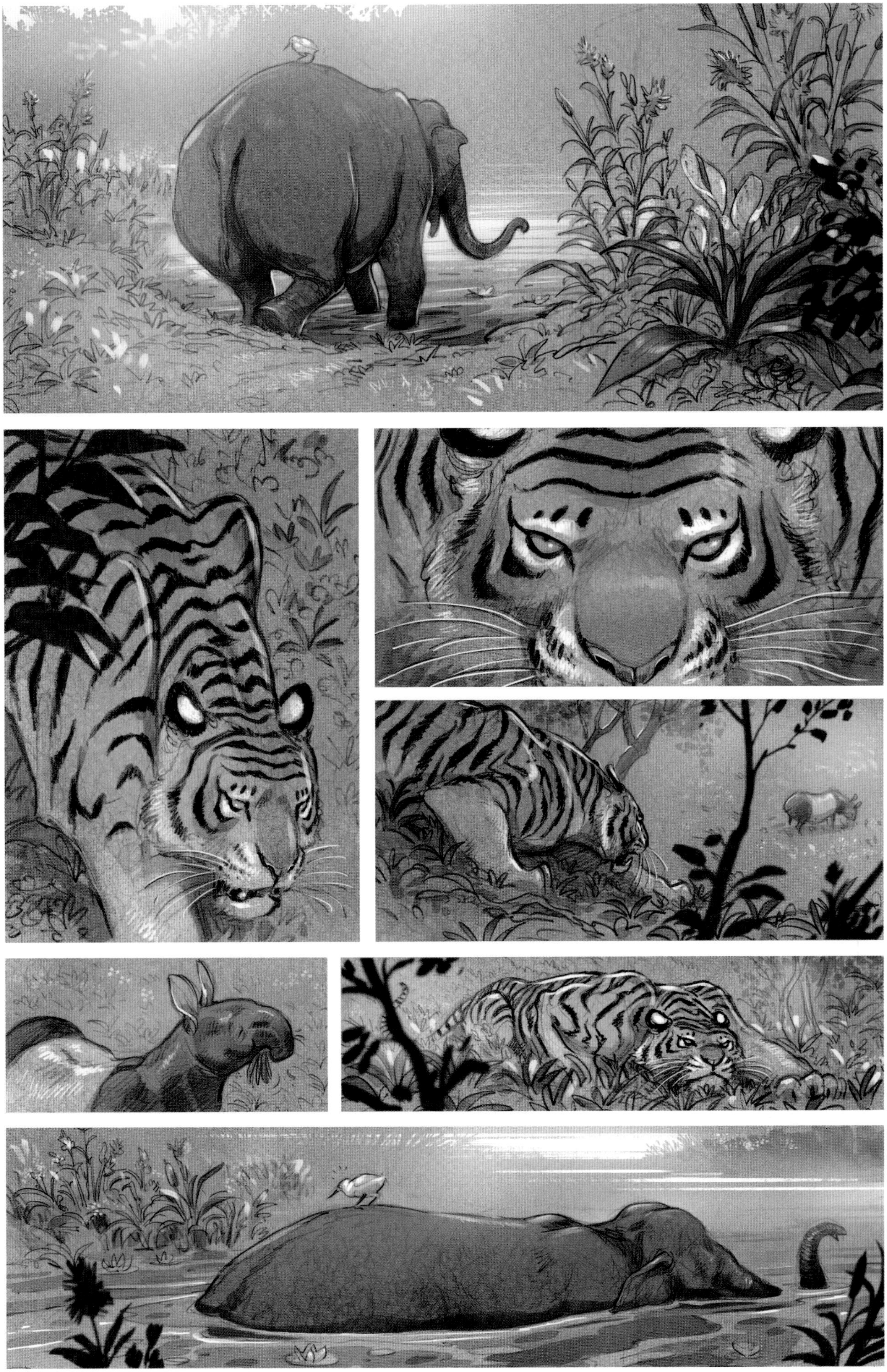

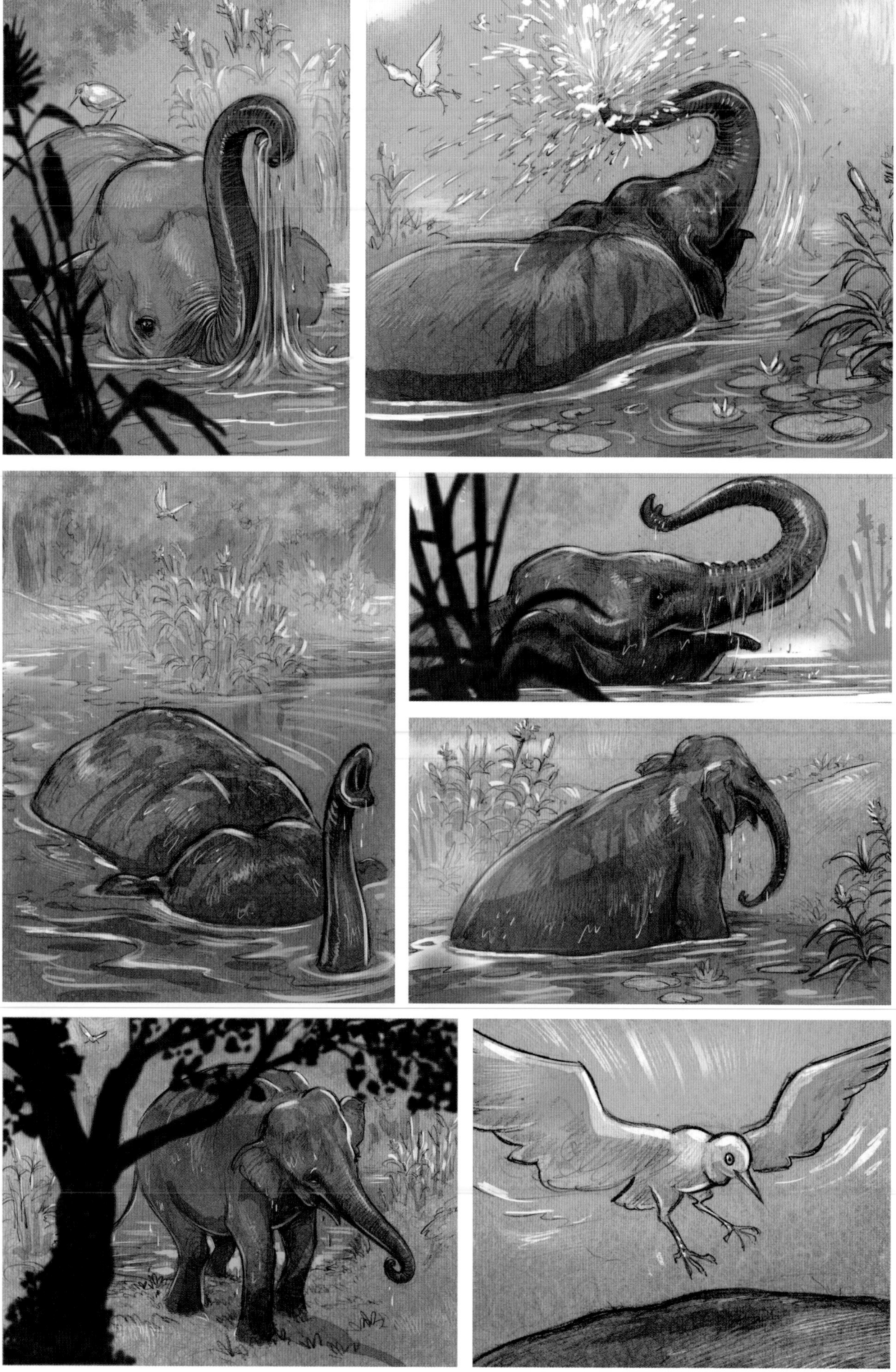

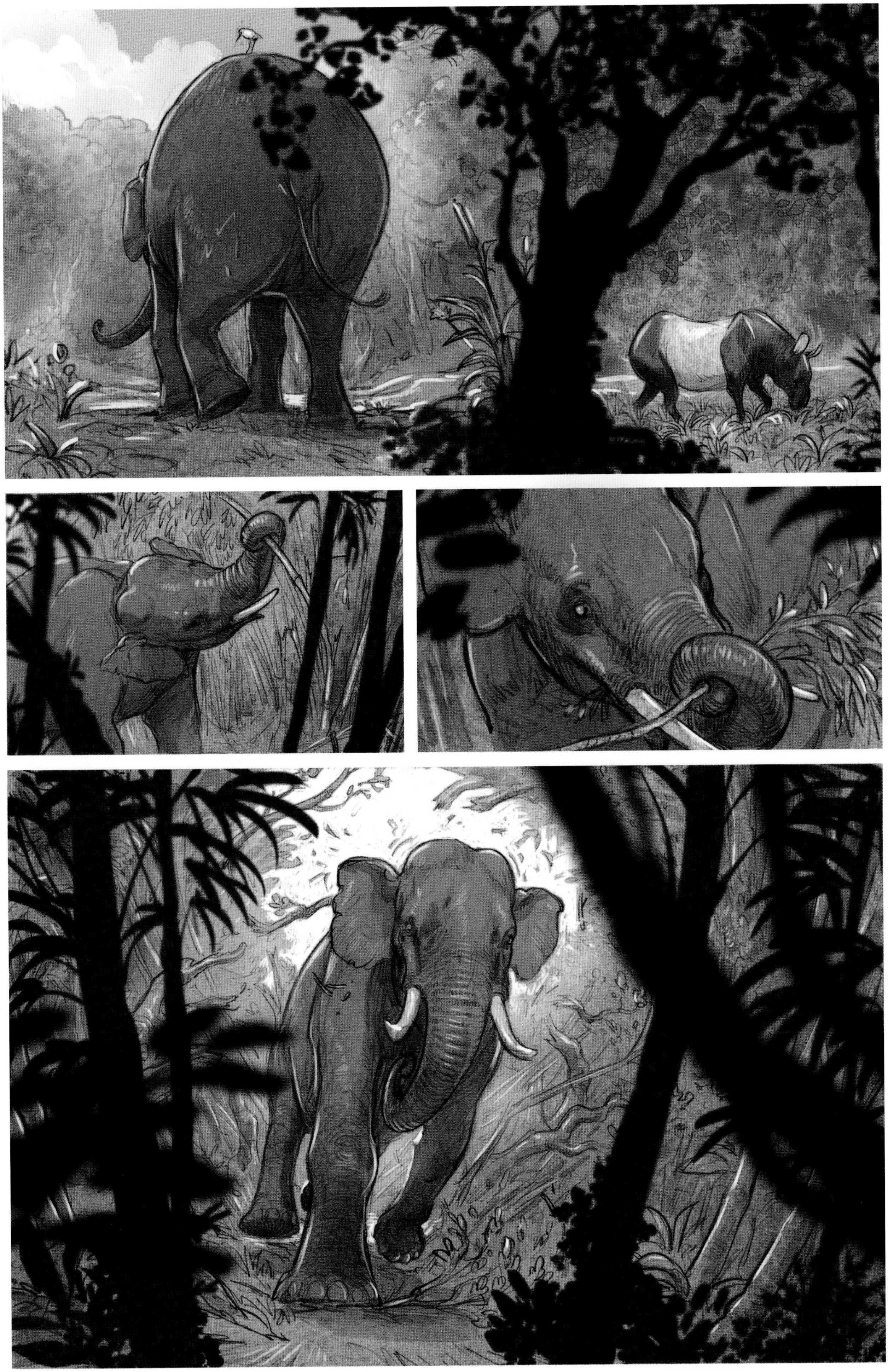

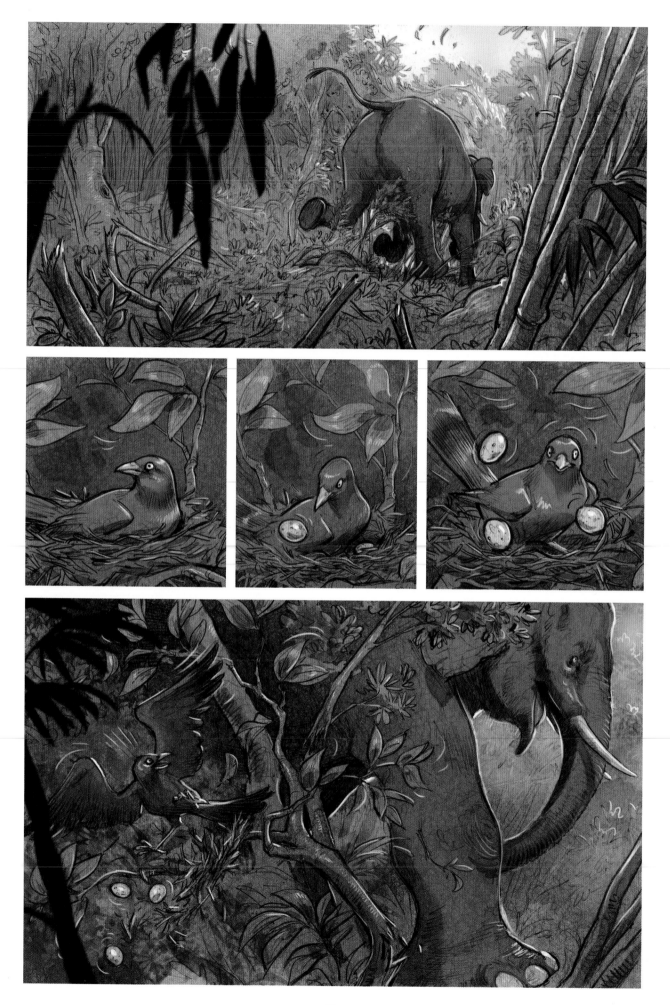

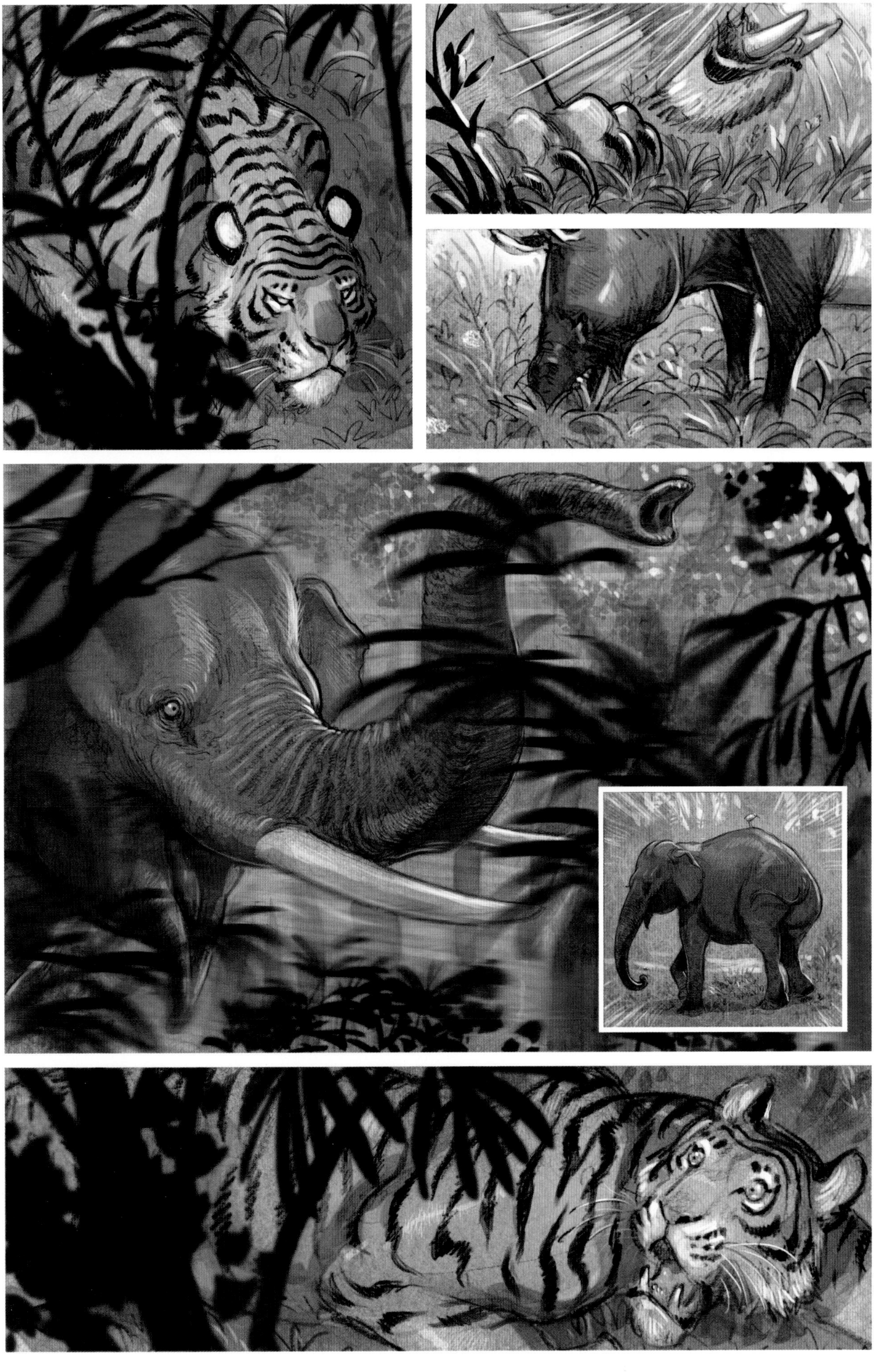

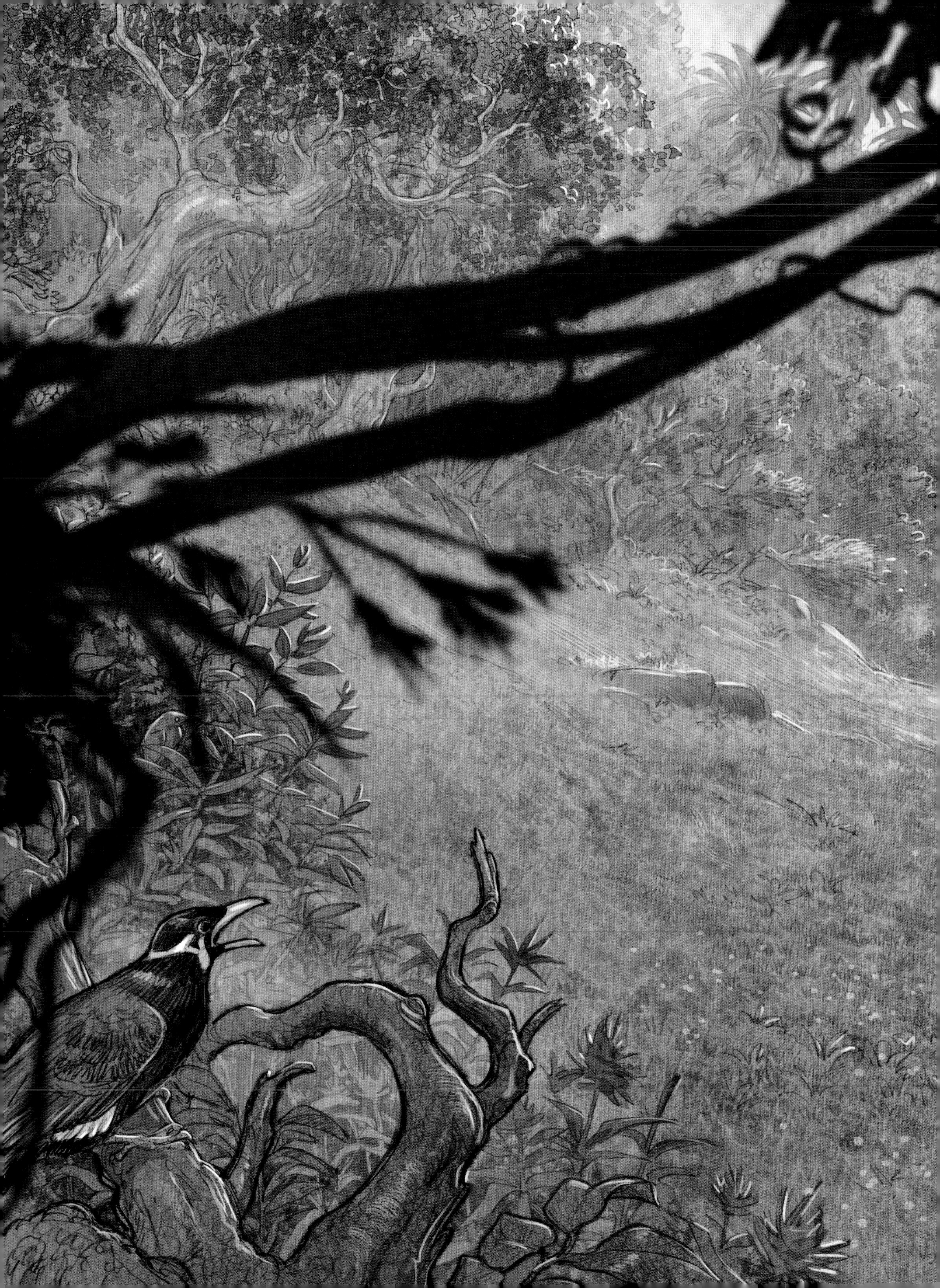

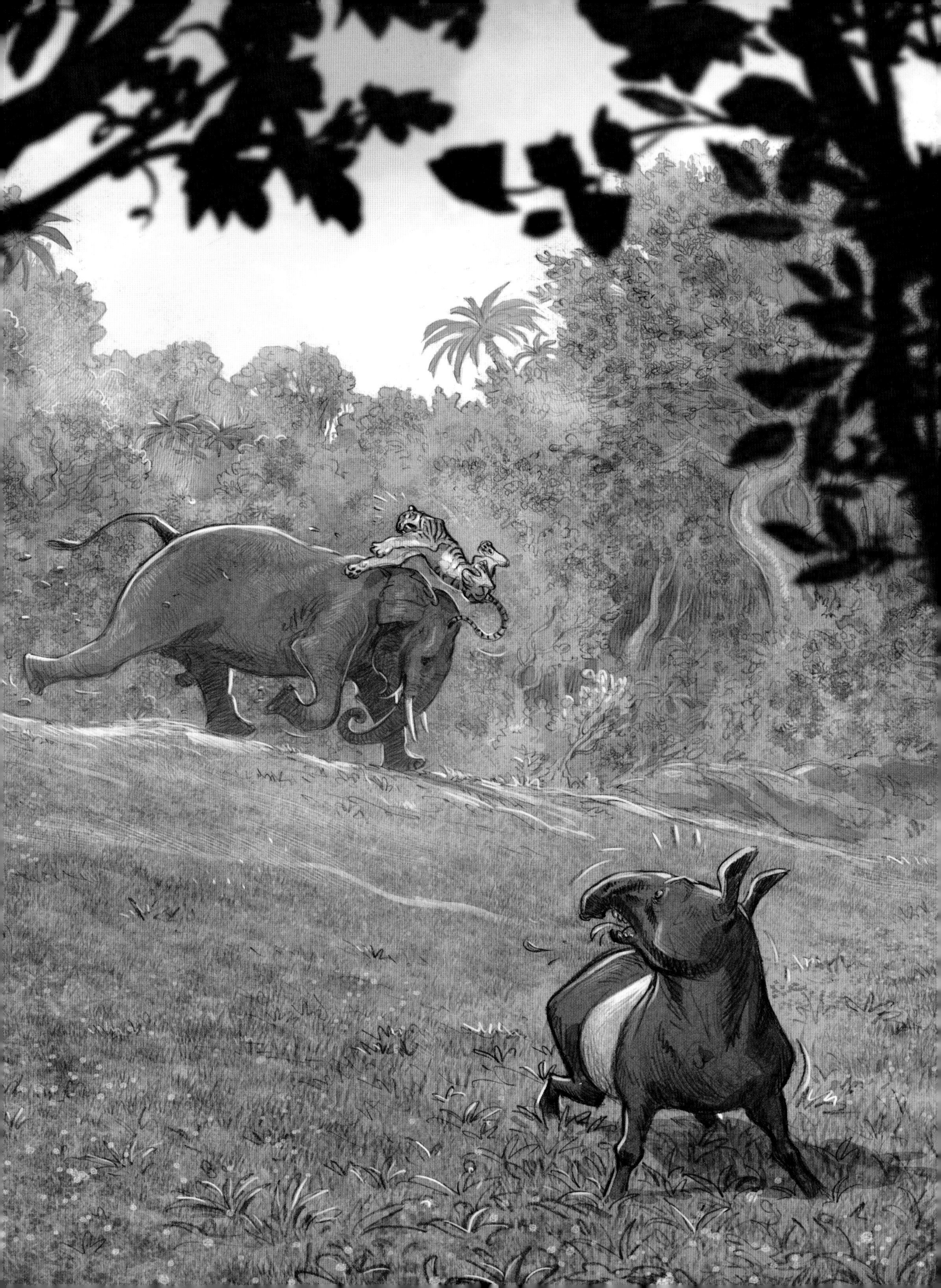

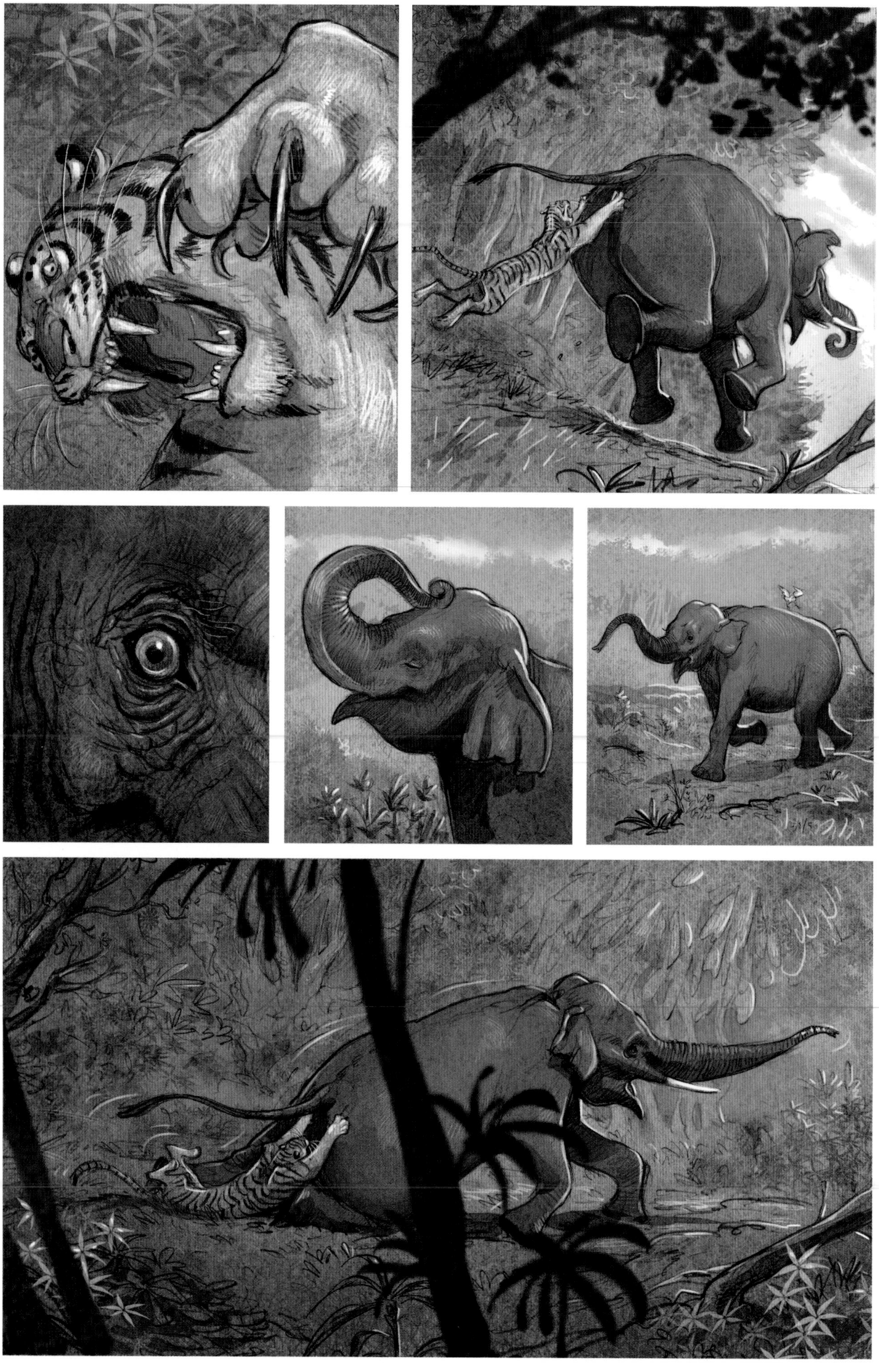

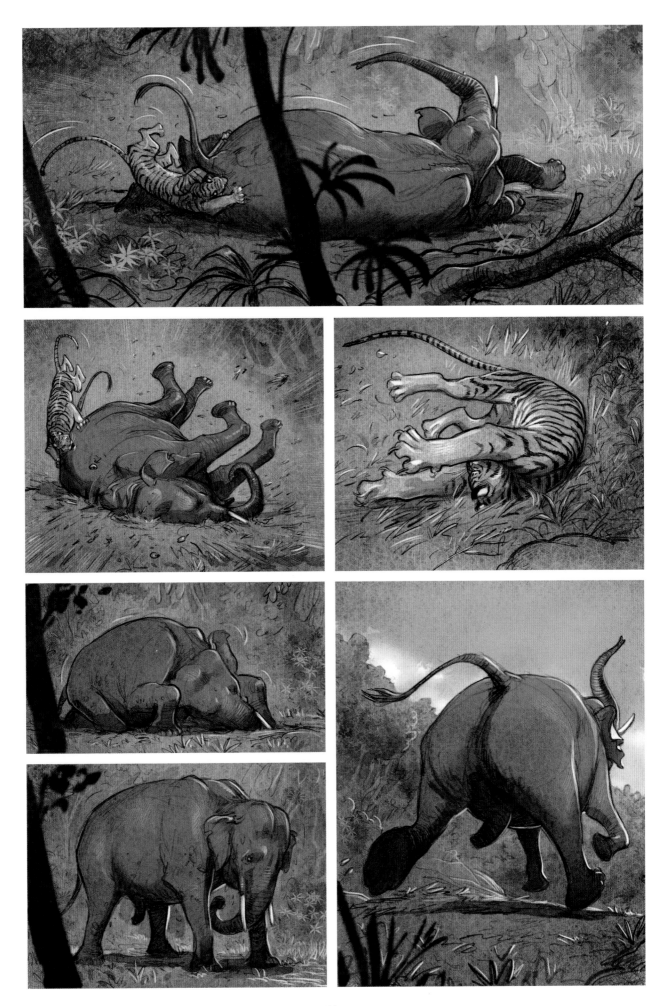

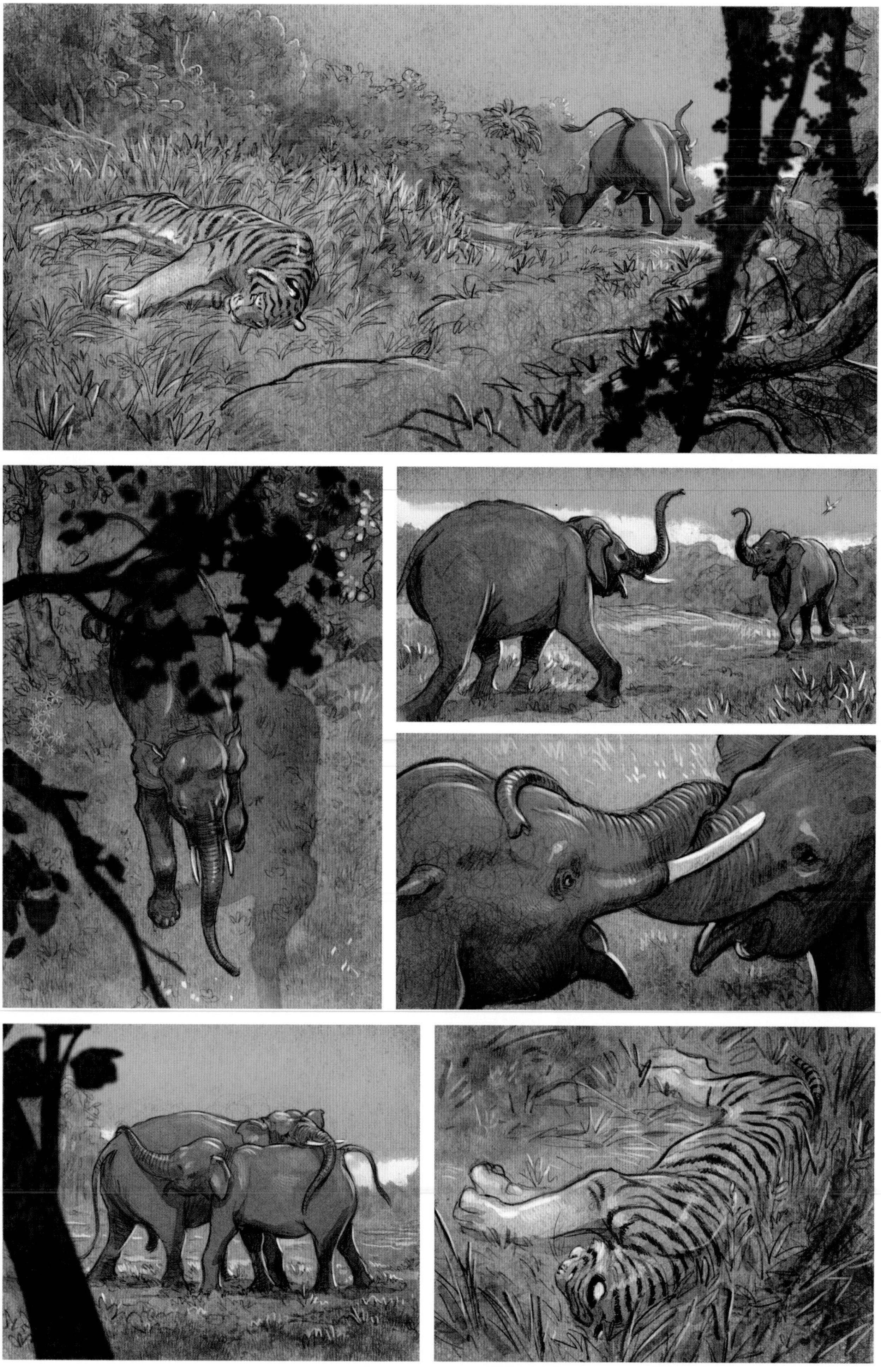

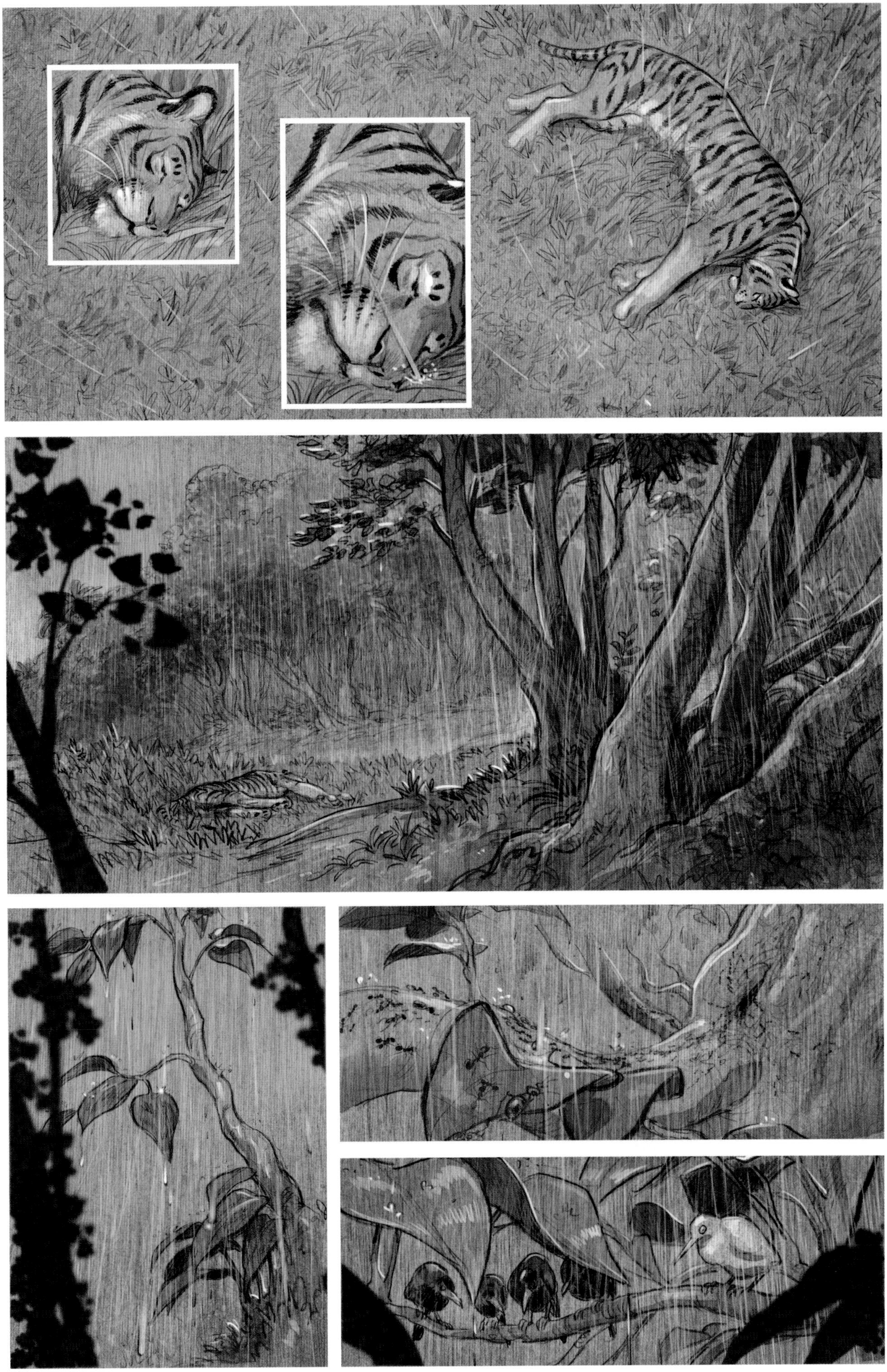

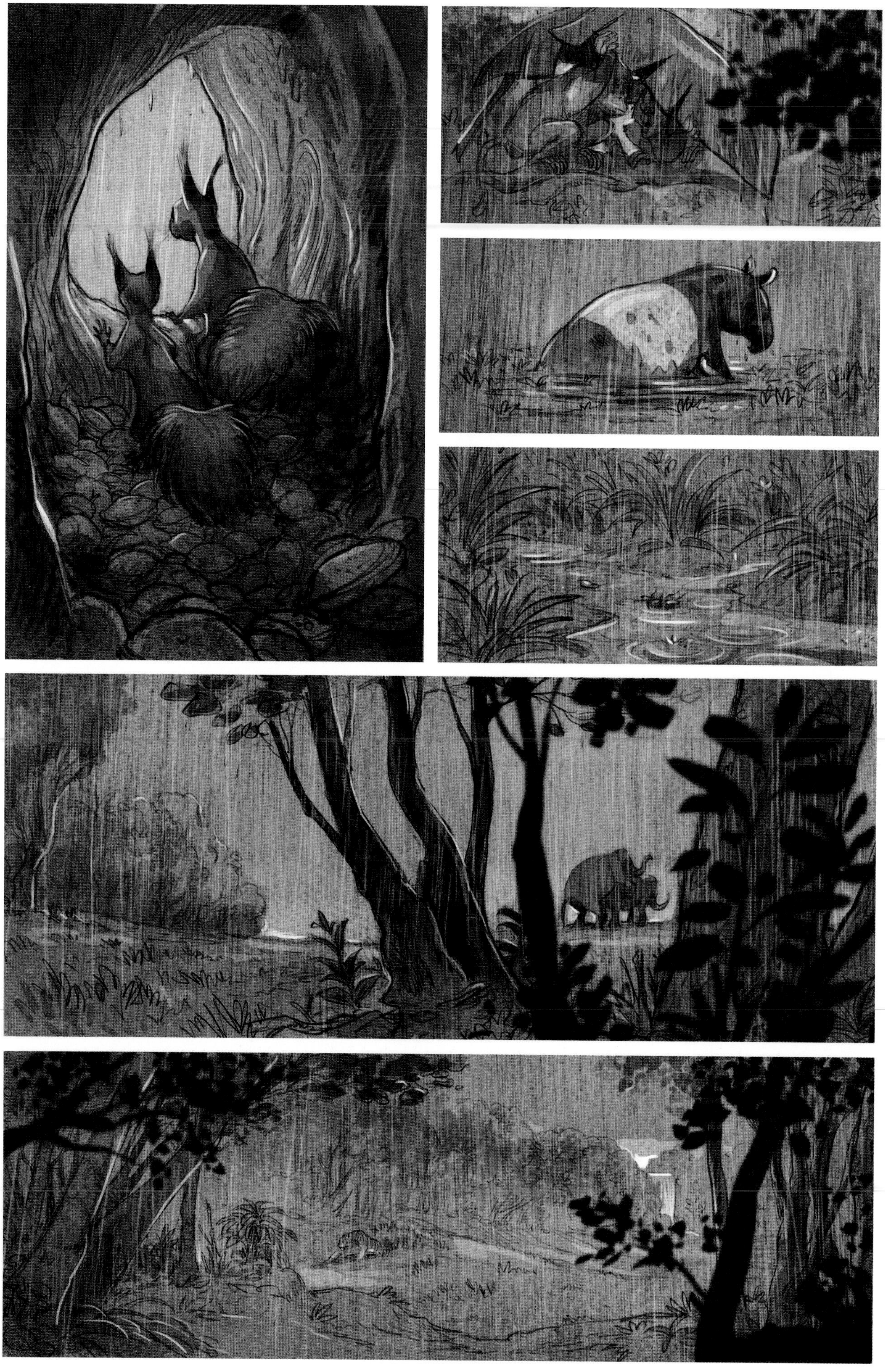

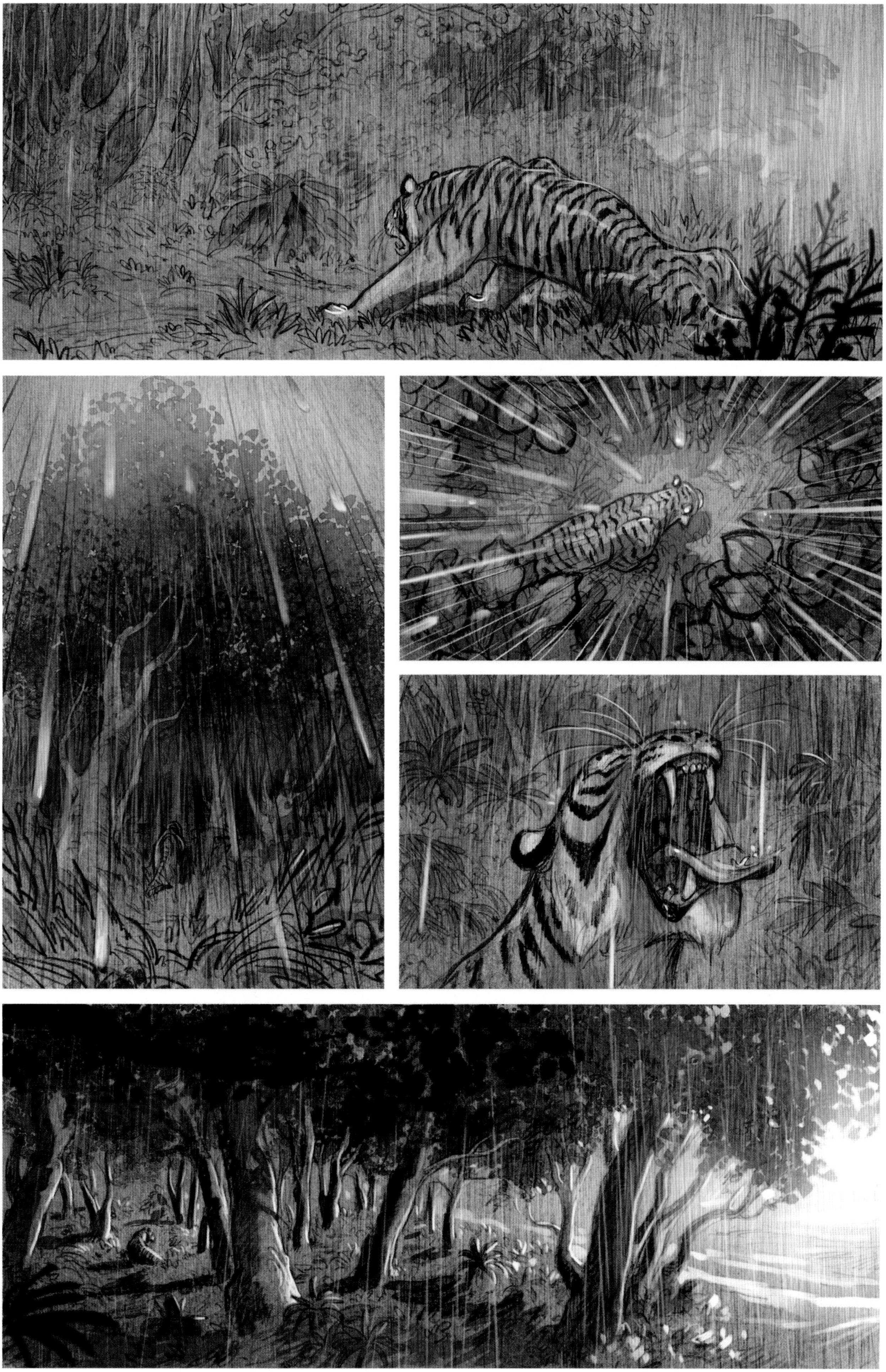

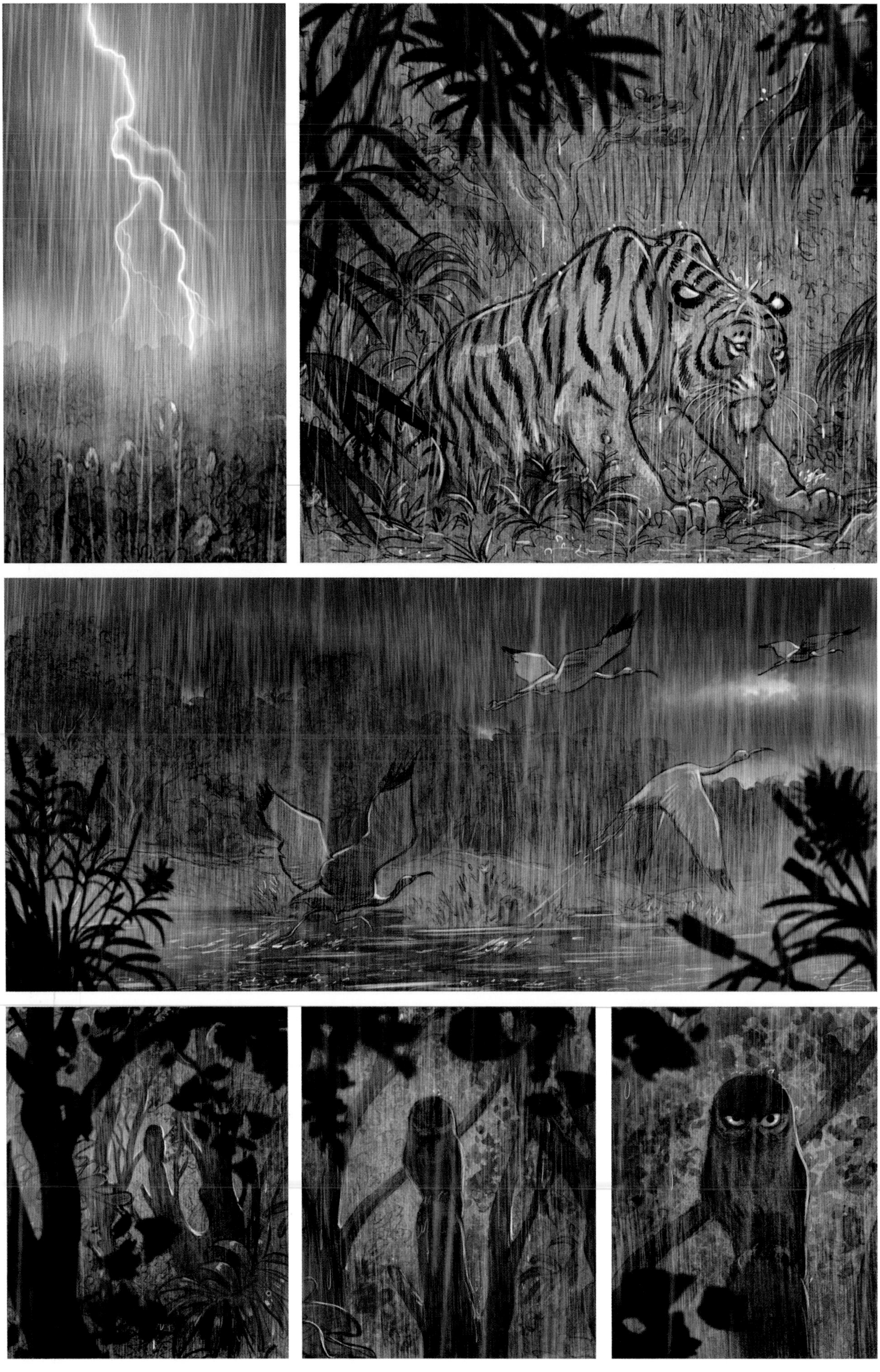

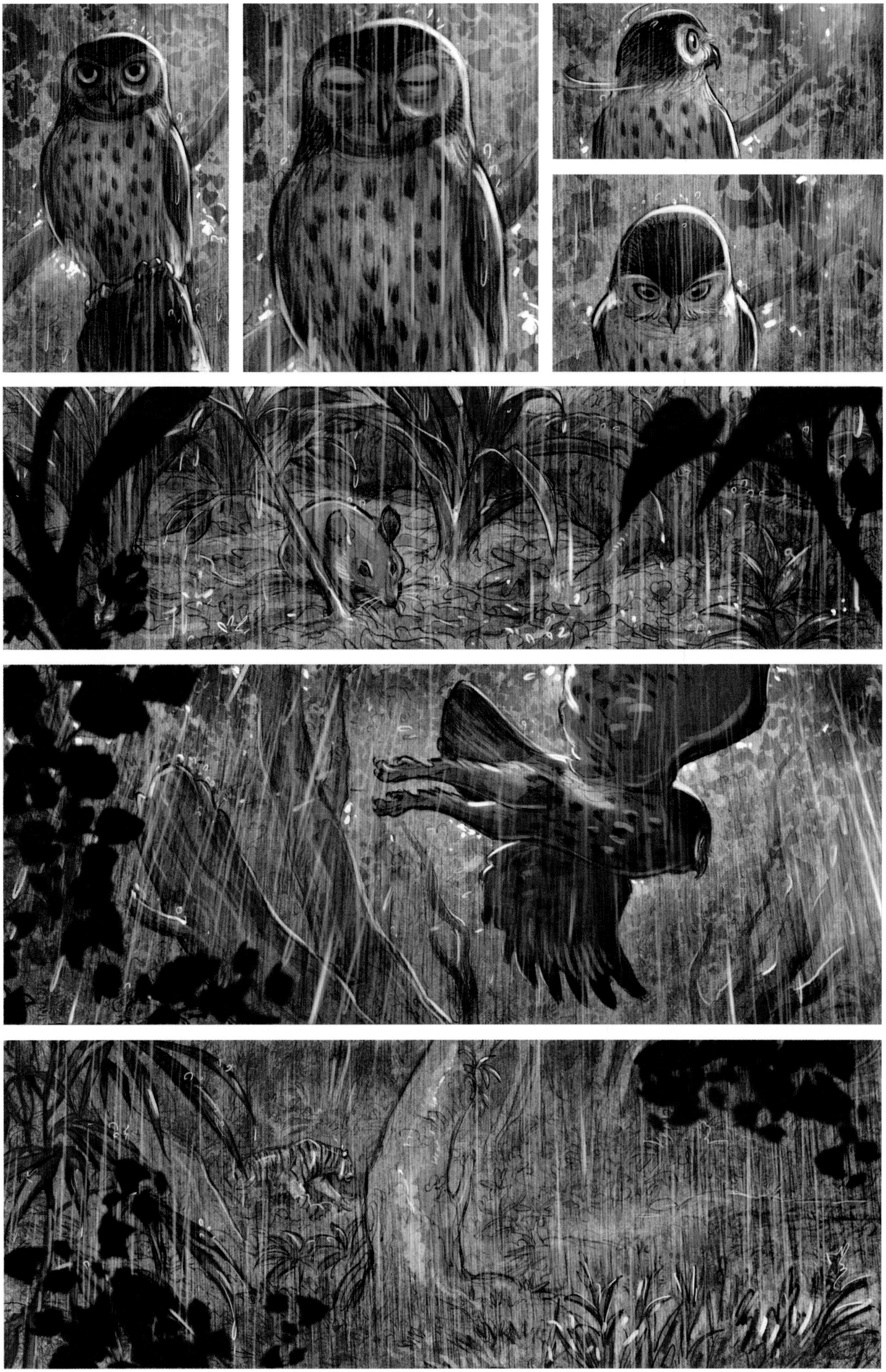

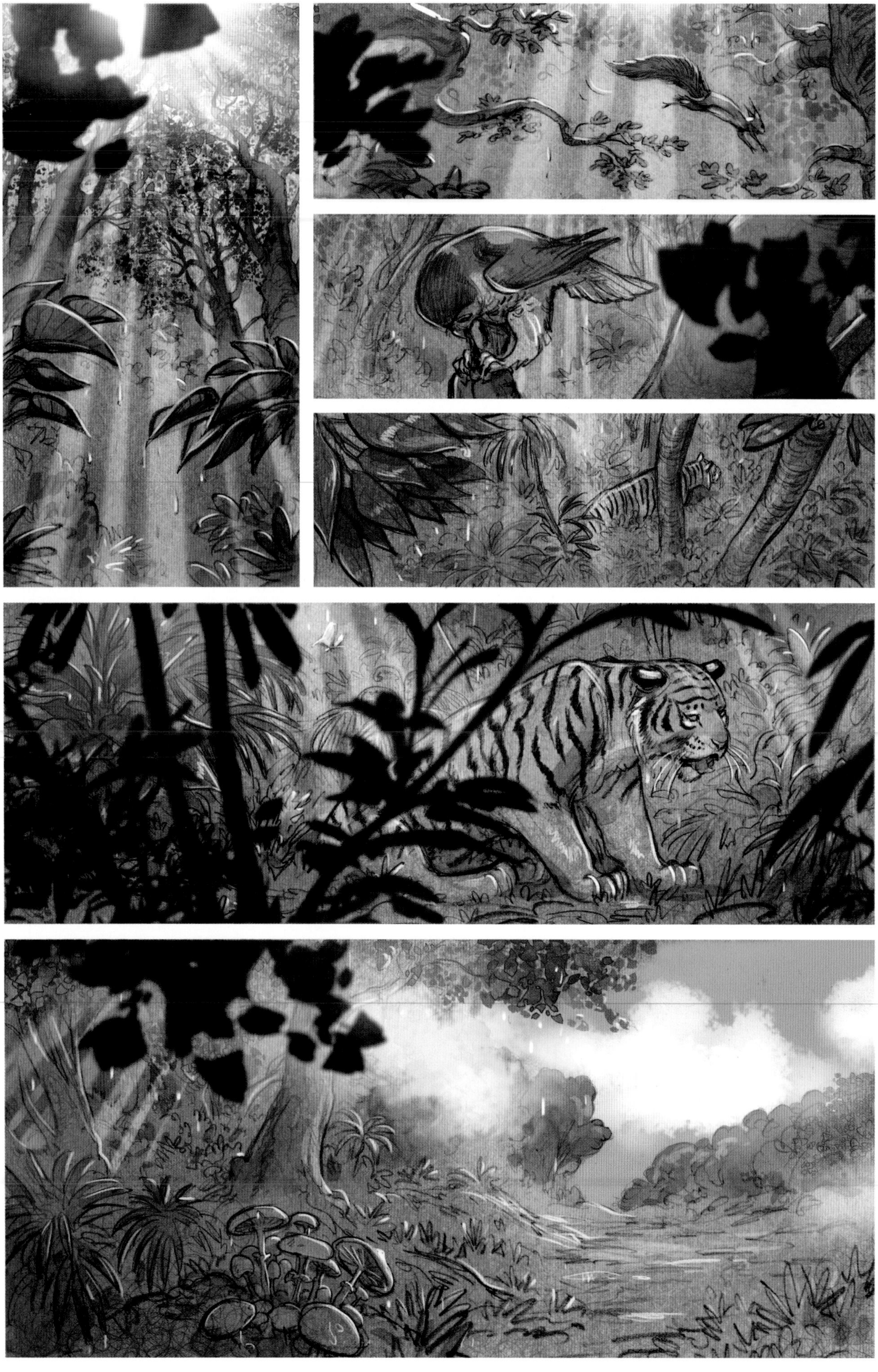

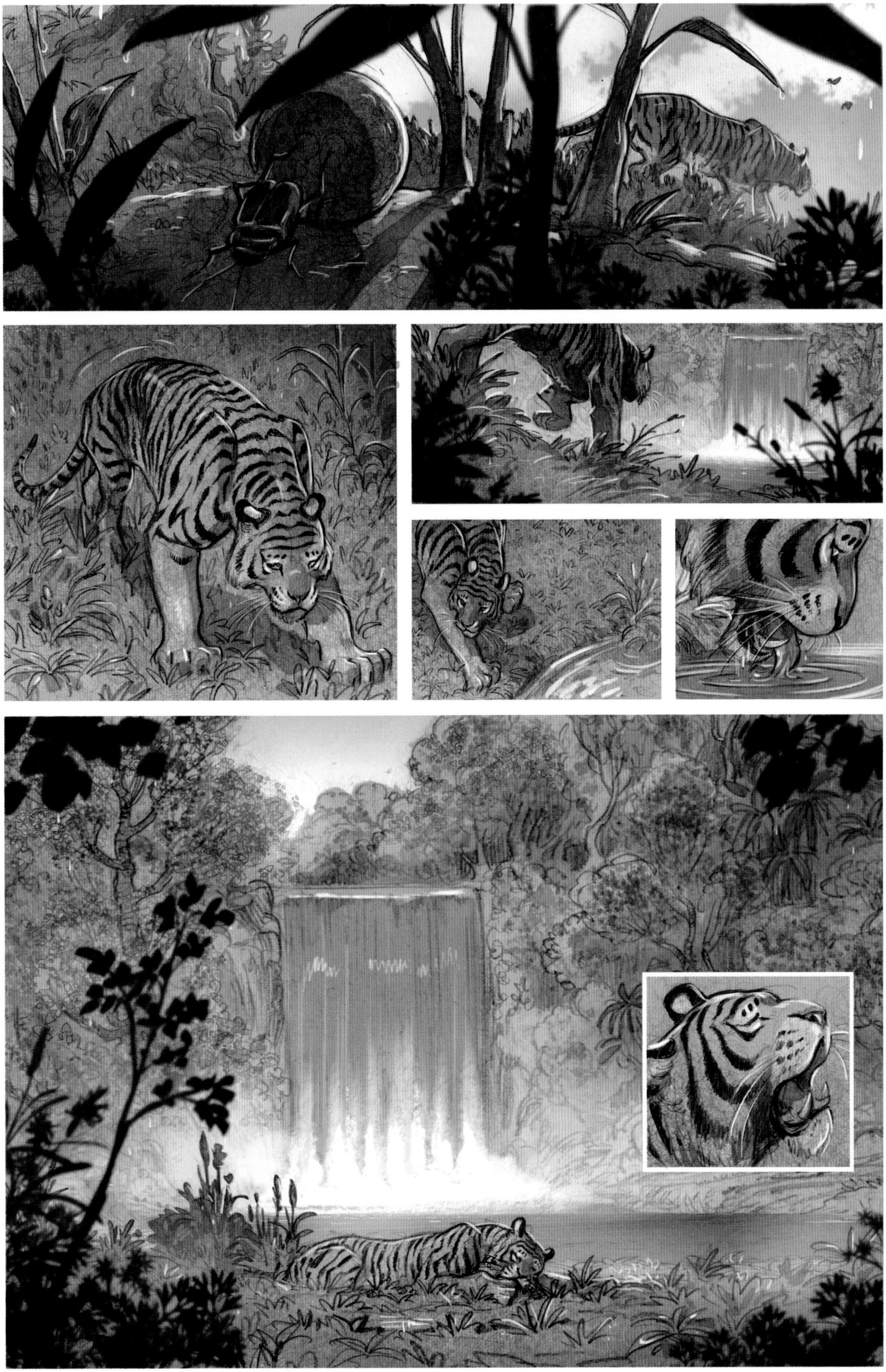

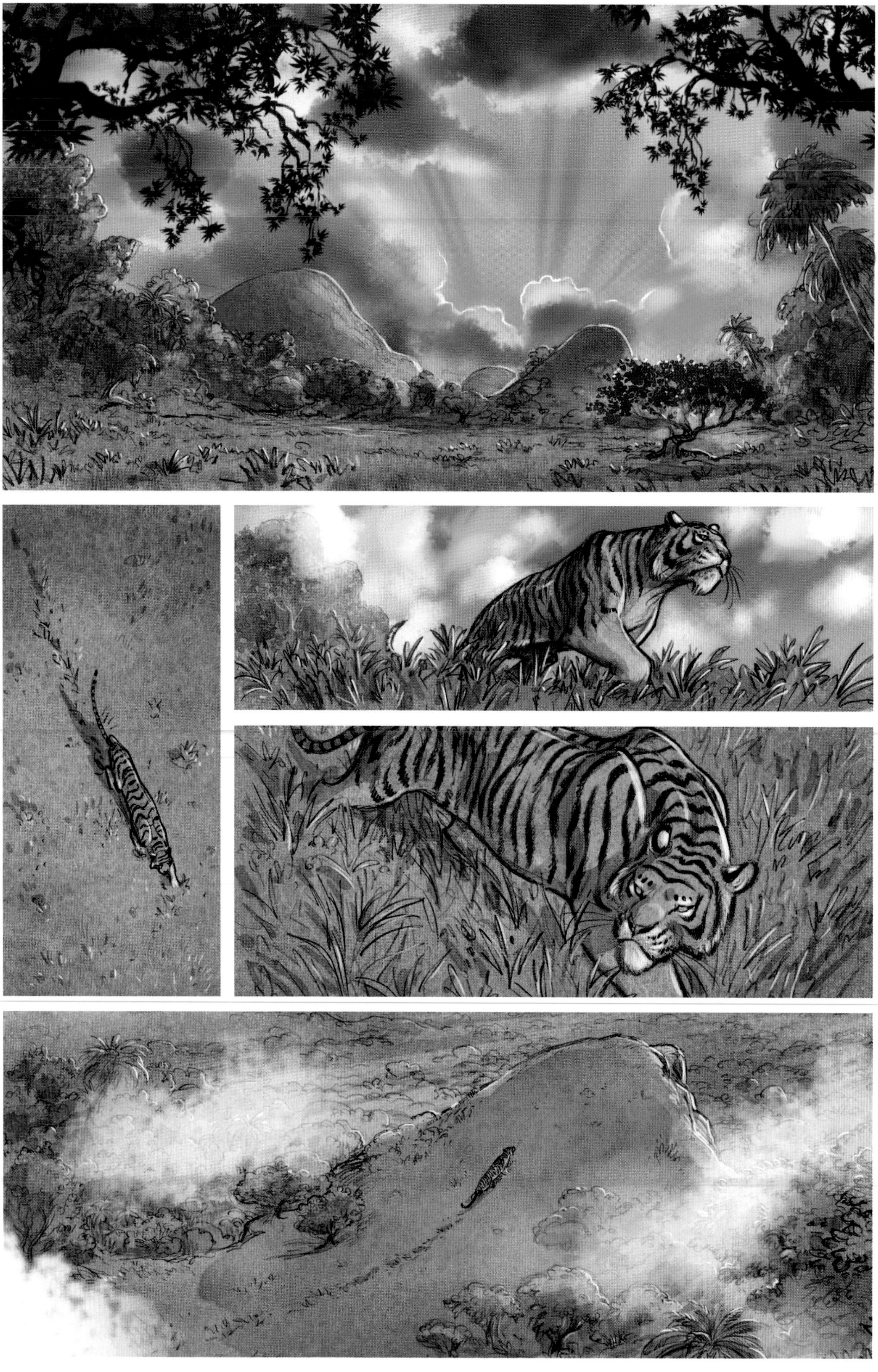

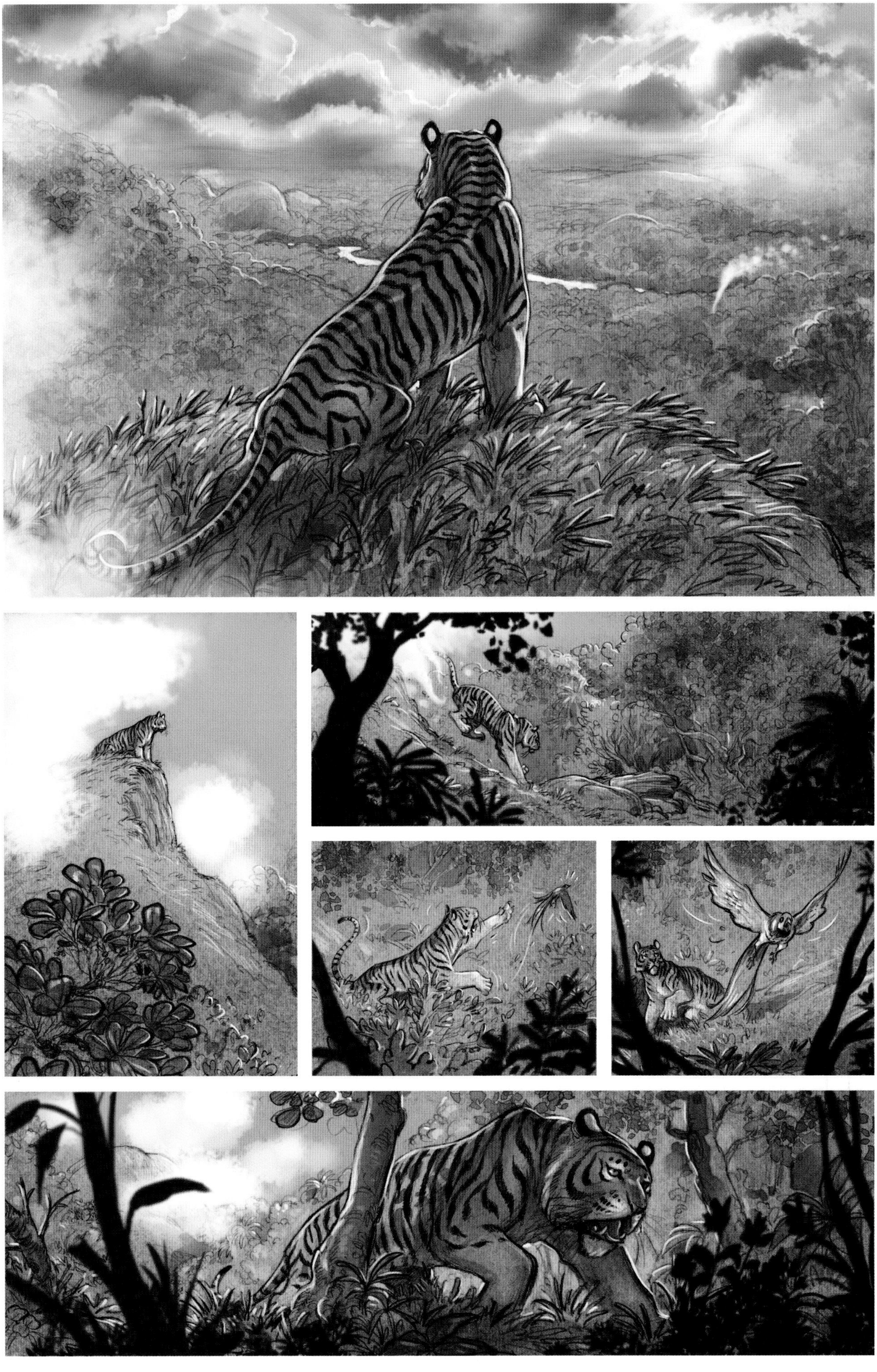

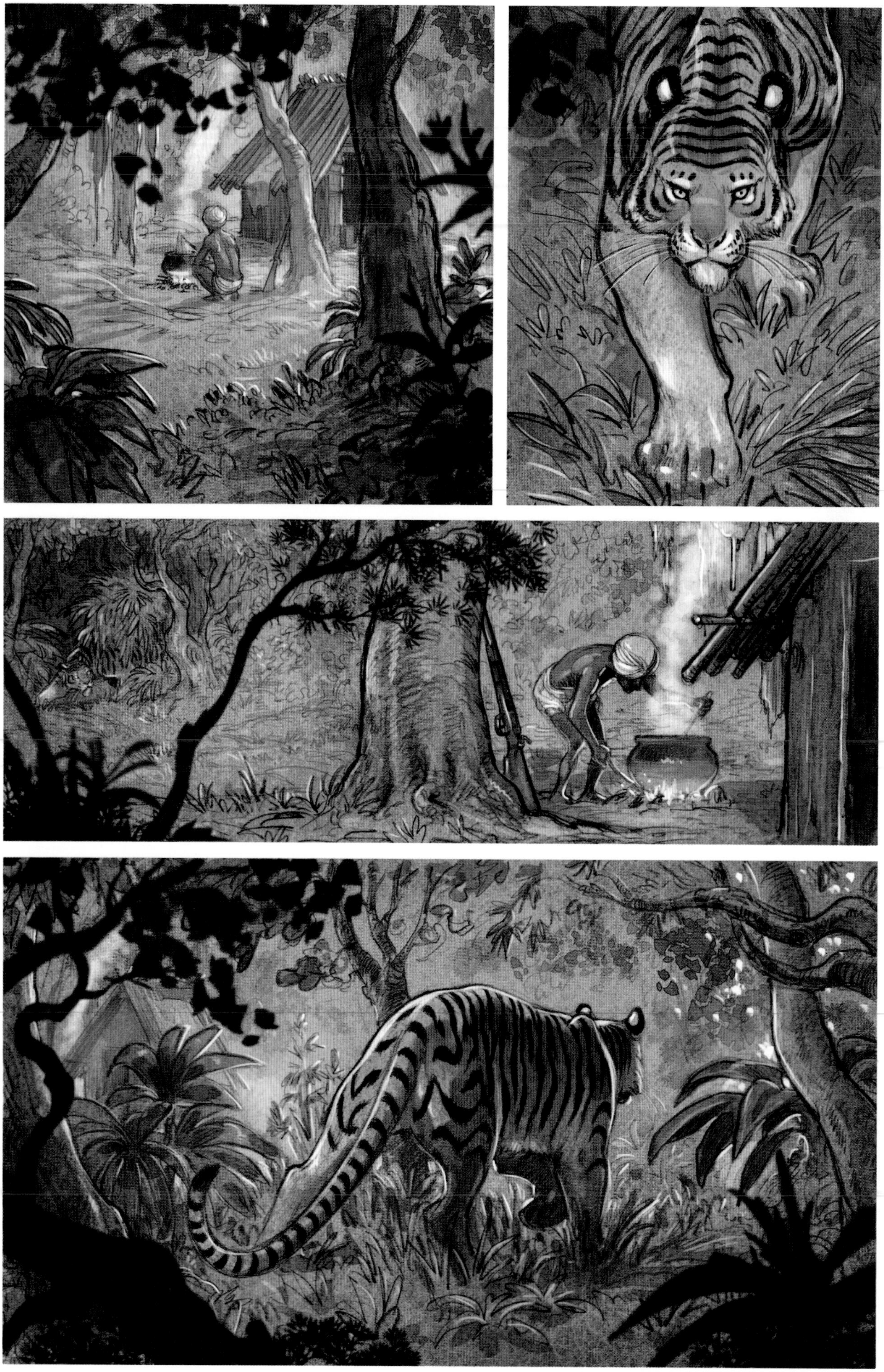

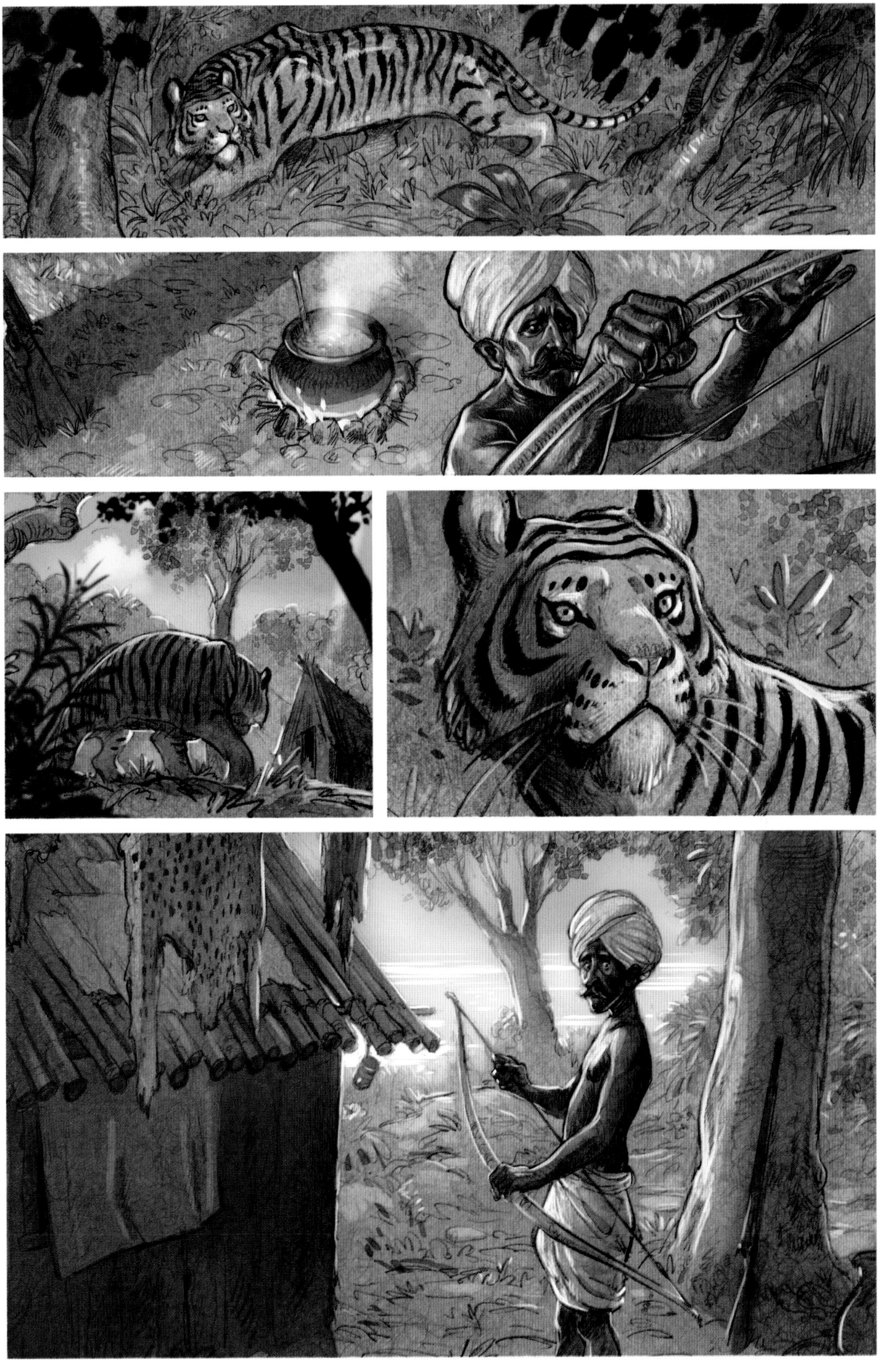

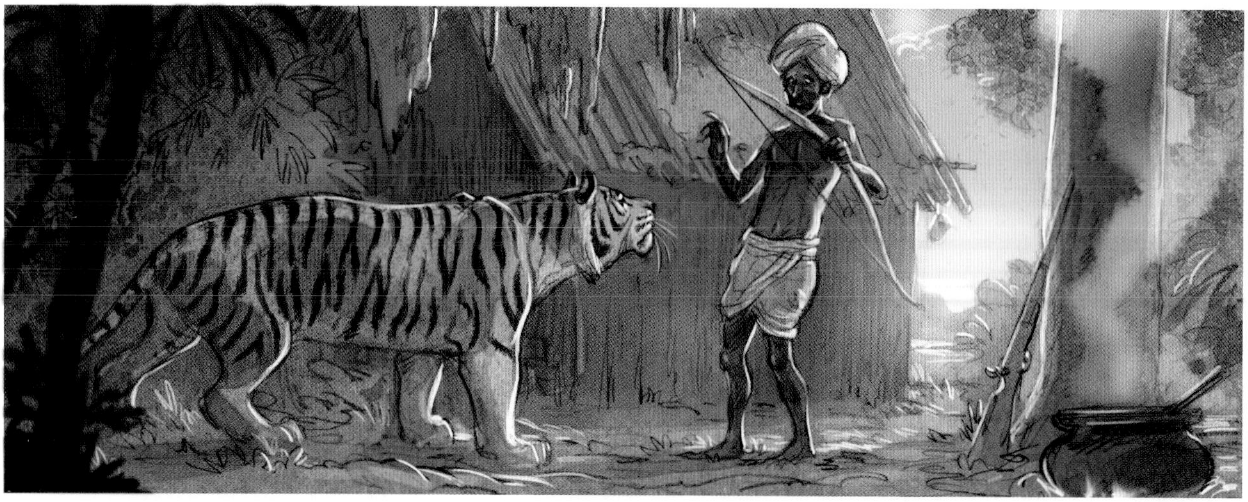
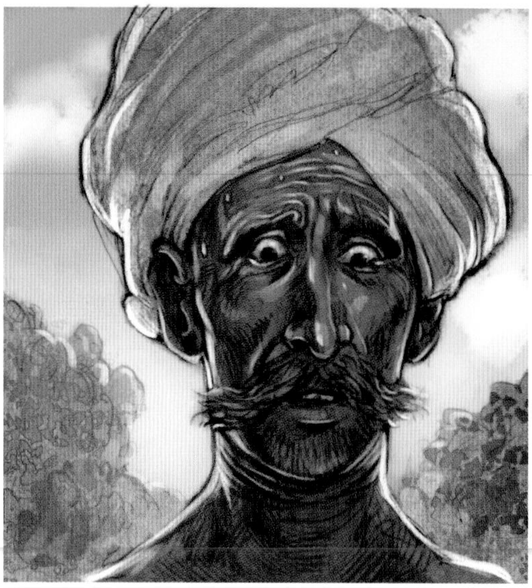
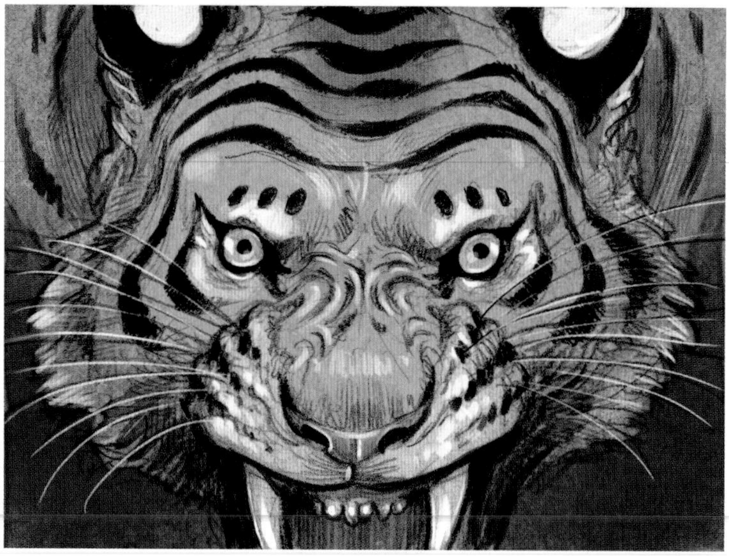
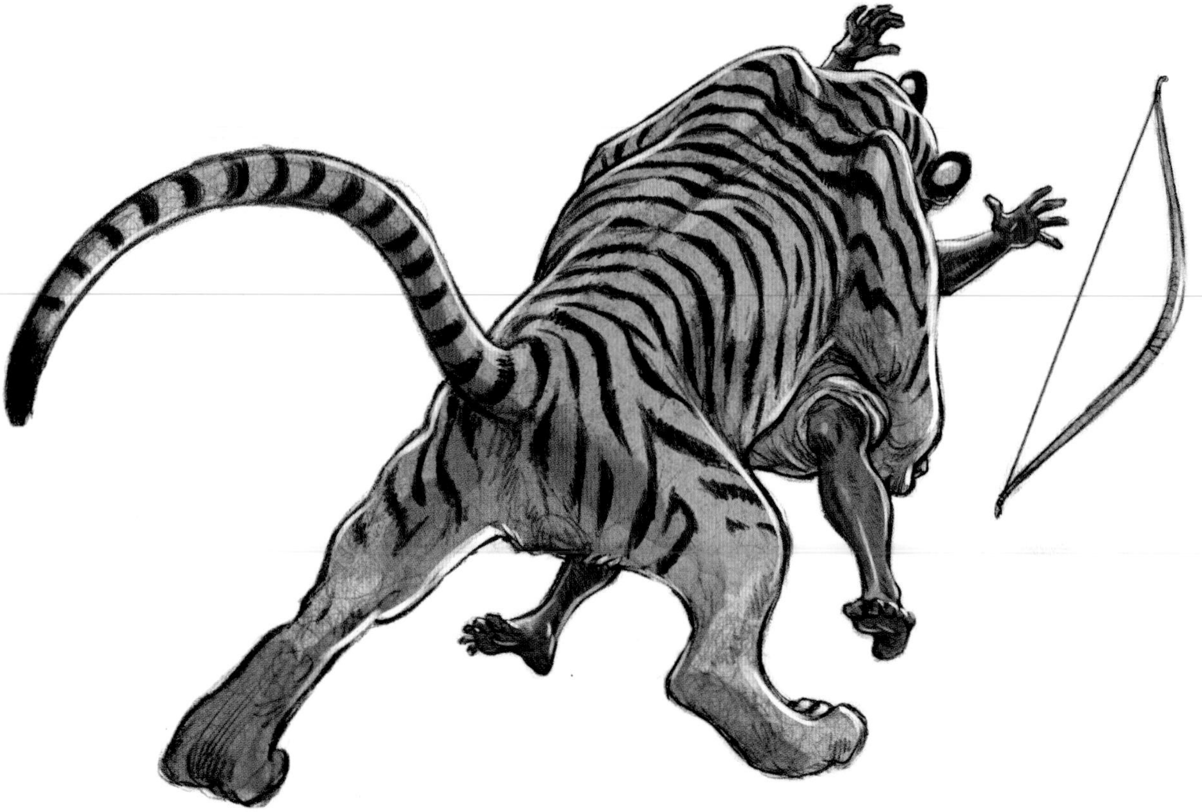

BECAUSE THIS BEAST, FOR WHICH THOU CRIEST,
LET'S NO MORTAL PASS BY, BUT SO HINDERS HIM
THAT HE WOULD BE DEVOURED.

OF ITS NATURE, SO MALIGN AND CRUEL,
THAT ITS DISIRE IS NEVER SATED, AND EVEN AFTER
FEASTING SHE IS HUNGRIER THAN BEFORE.

THE DIVINE COMEDY,
DANTE ALIGHIERI

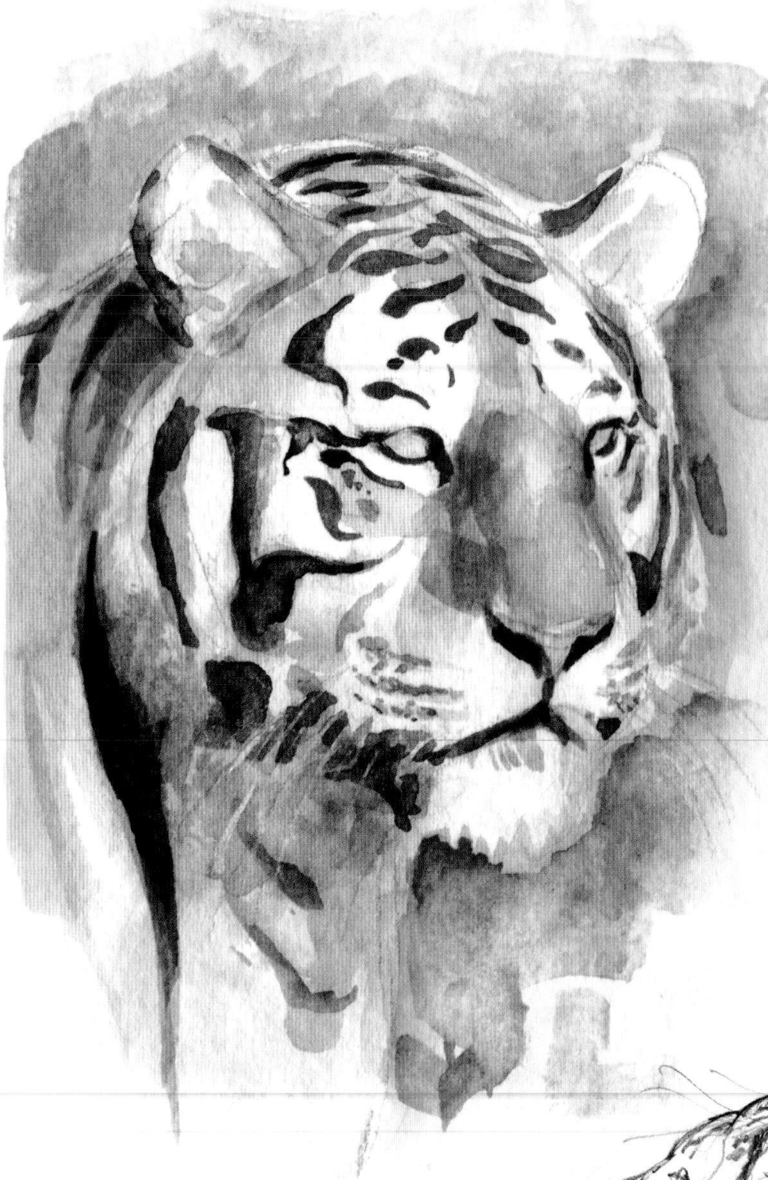

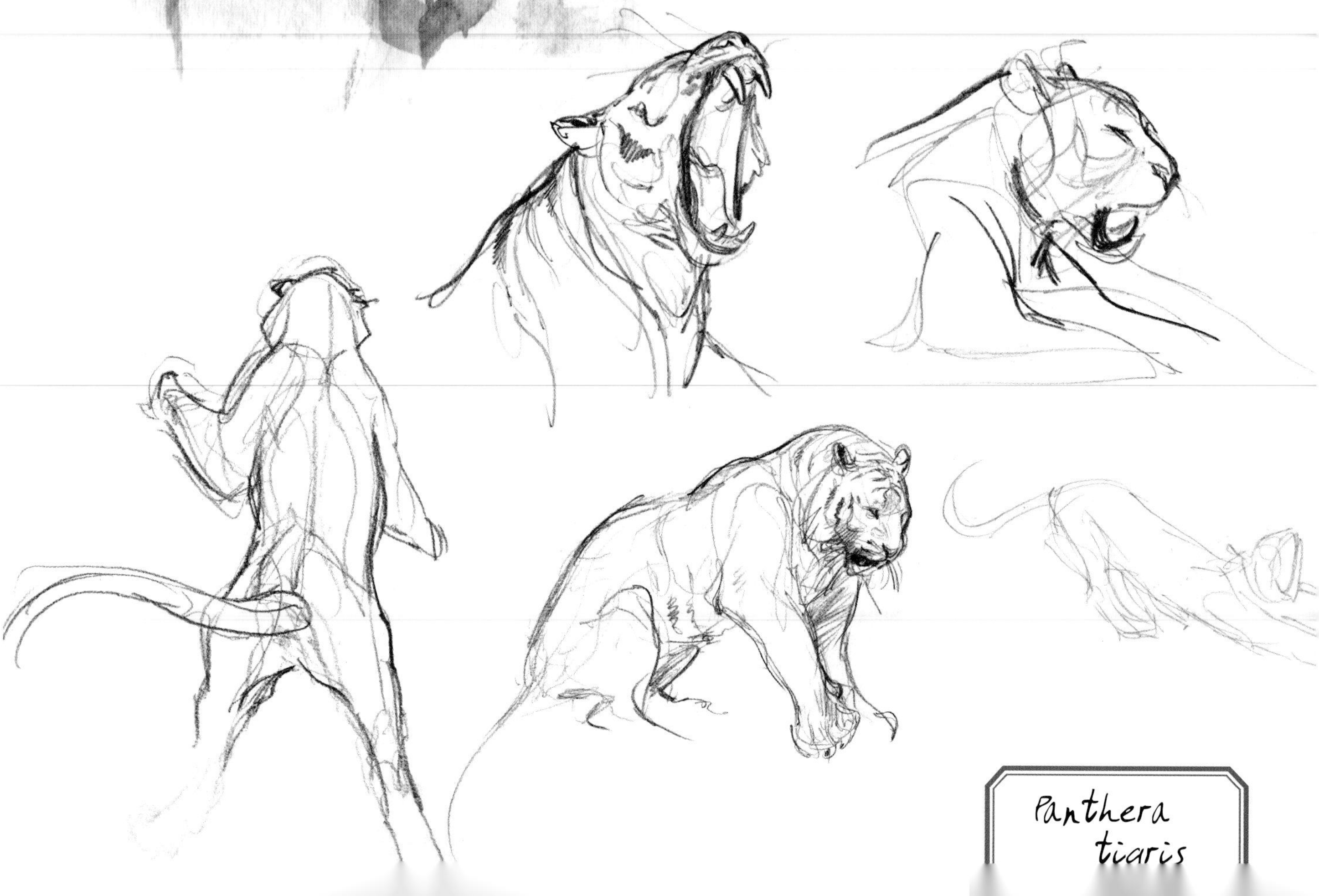
Panthera
tigris

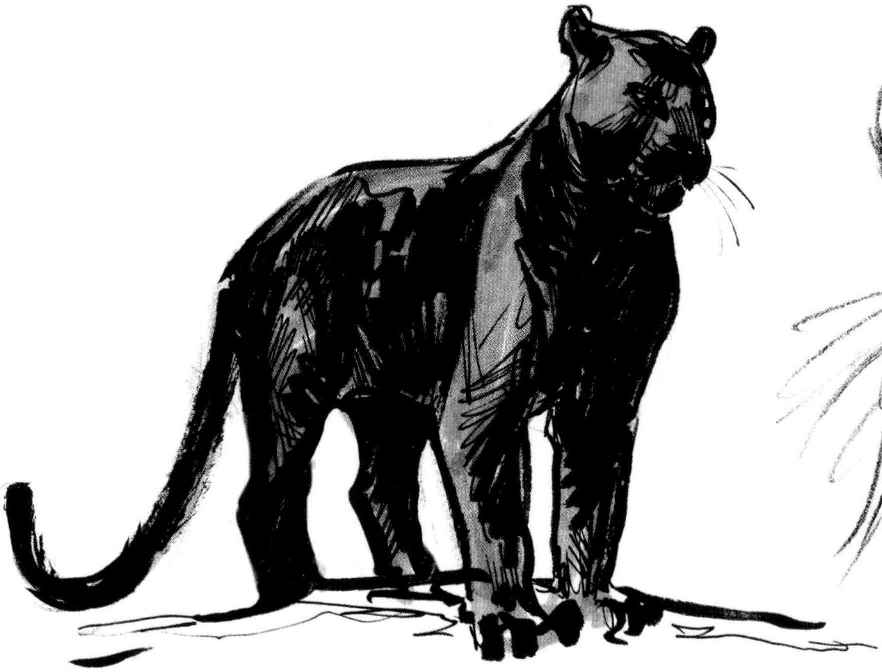

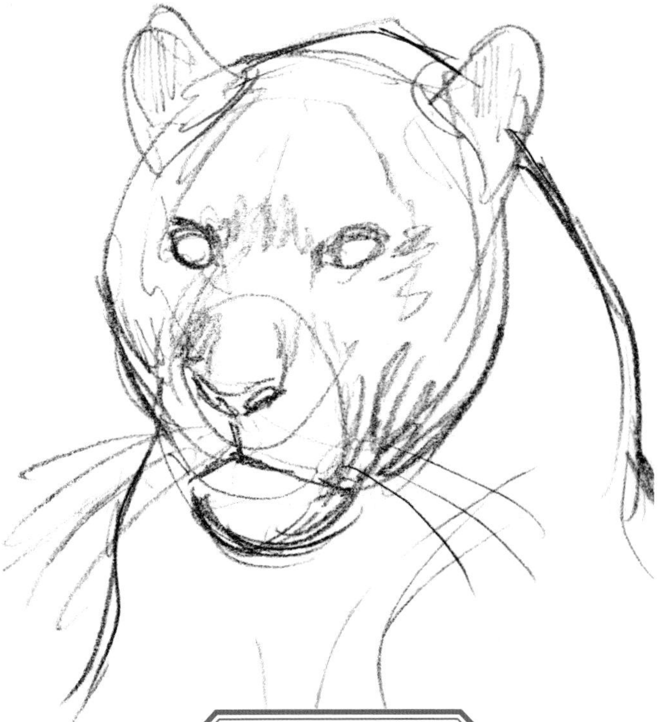

Panthera pardus

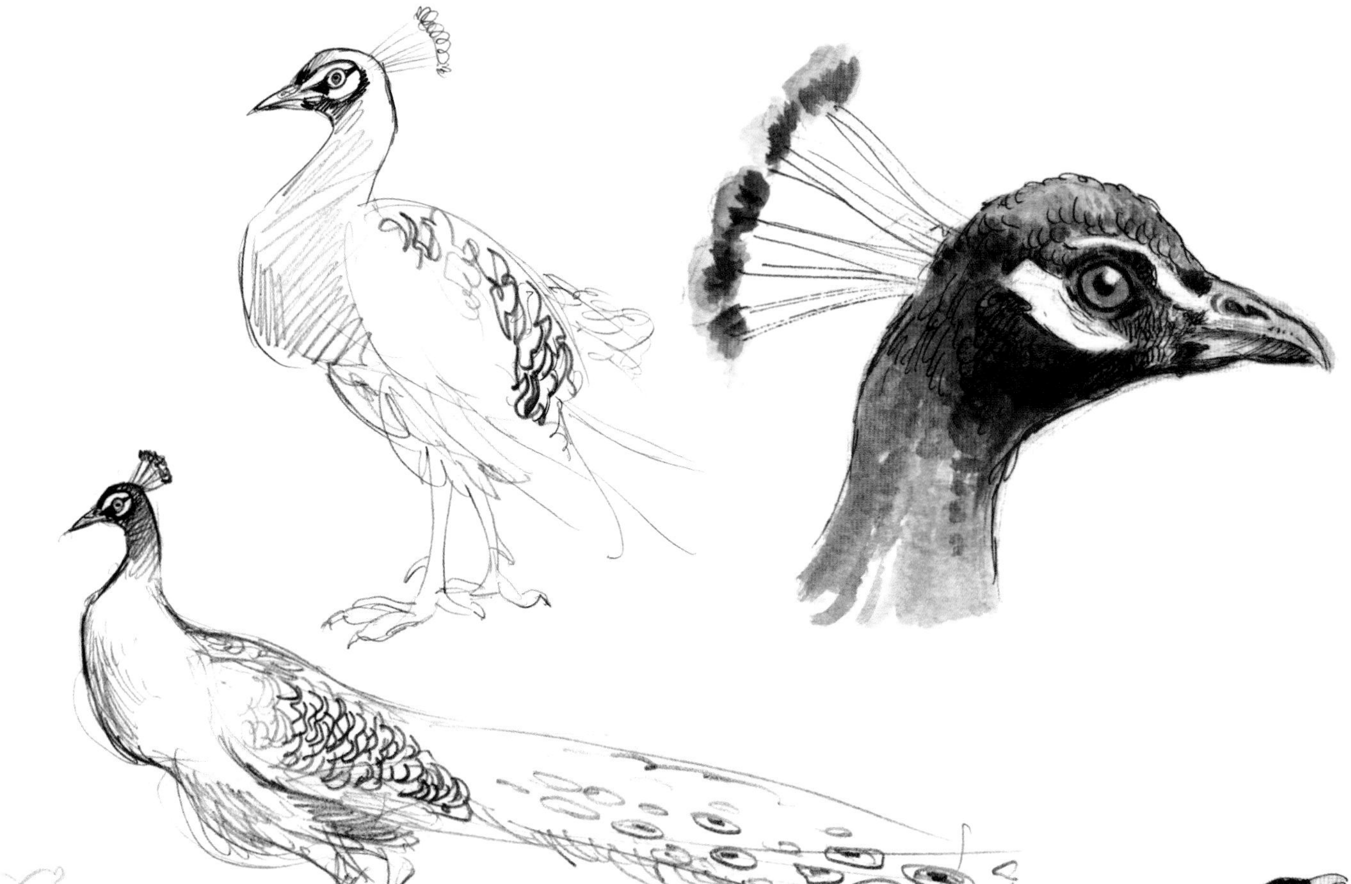

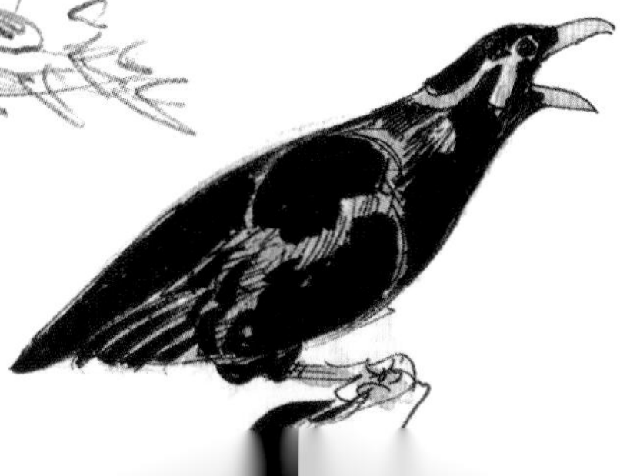

Avis

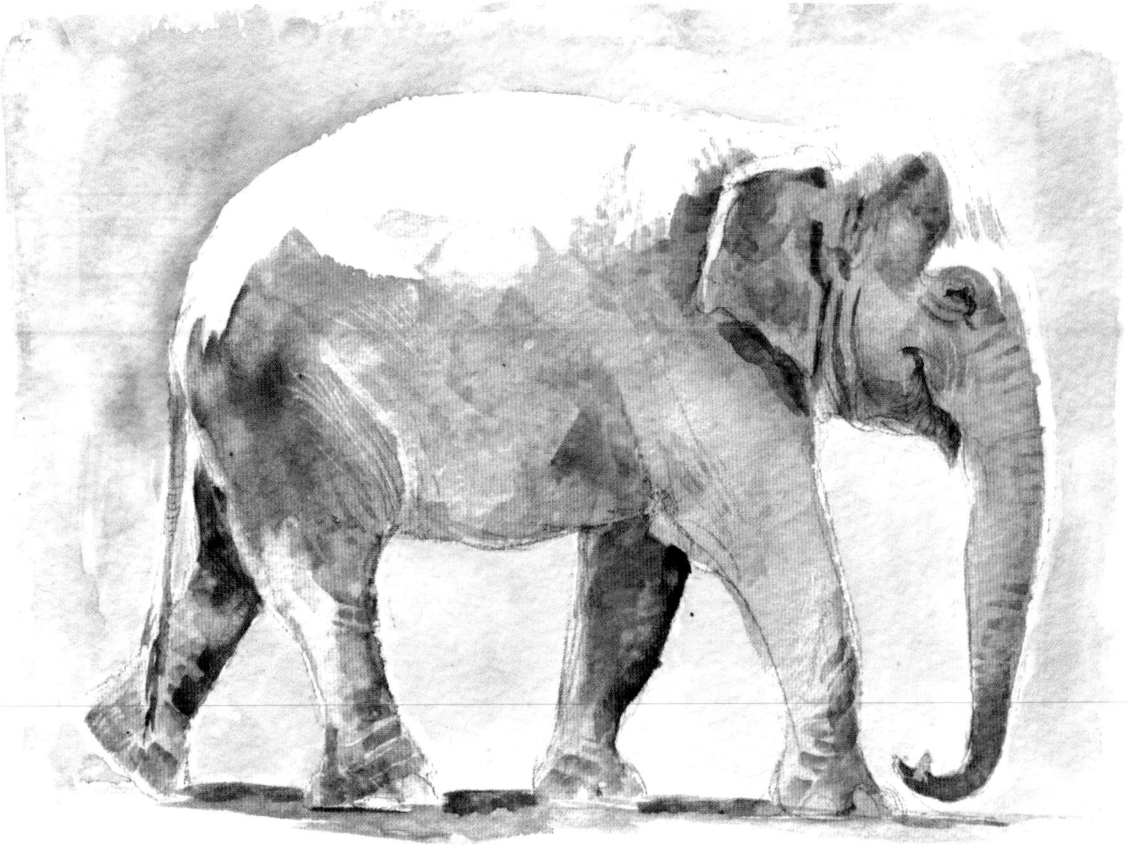

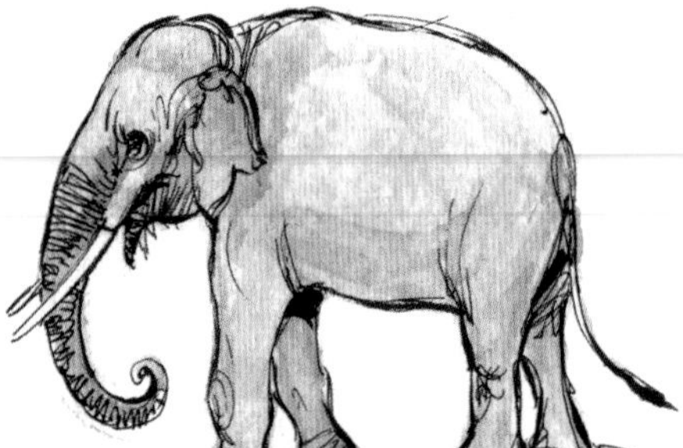

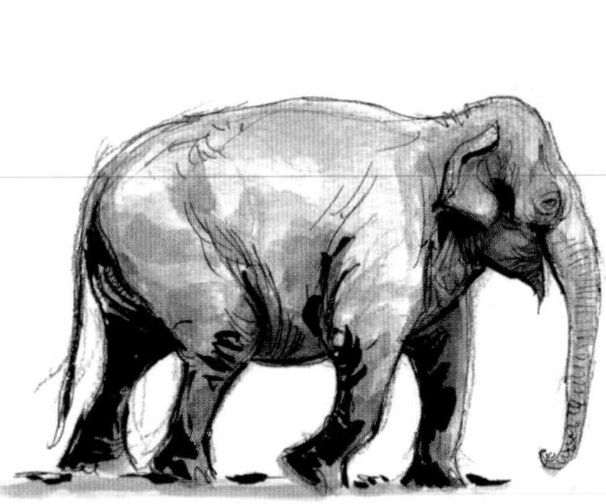

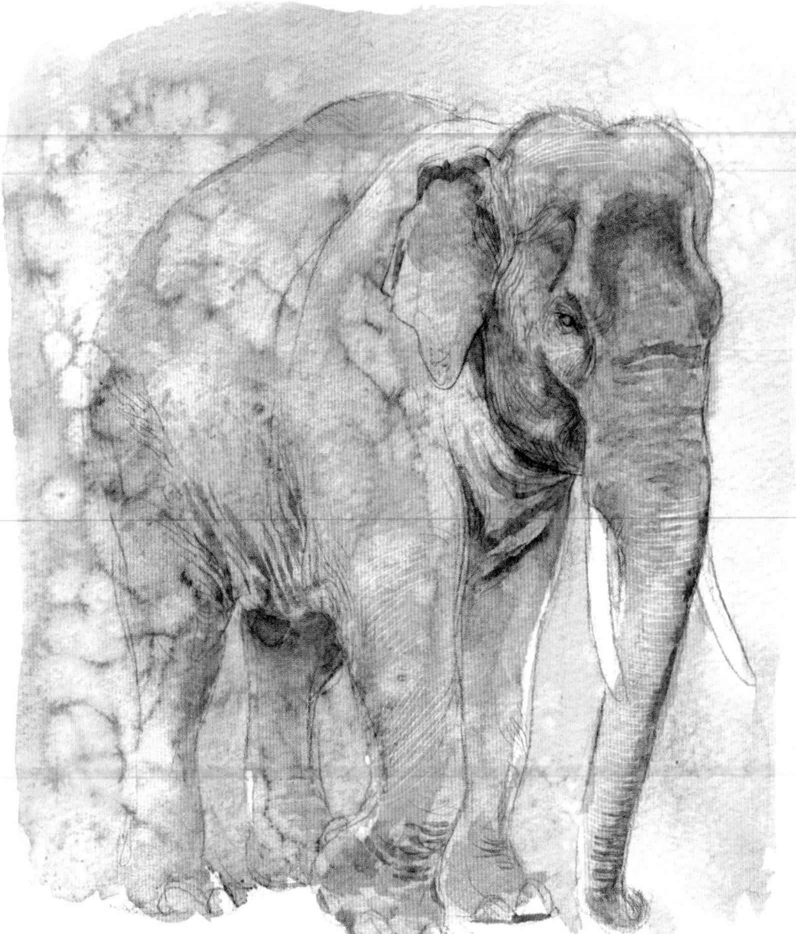

Elephantus

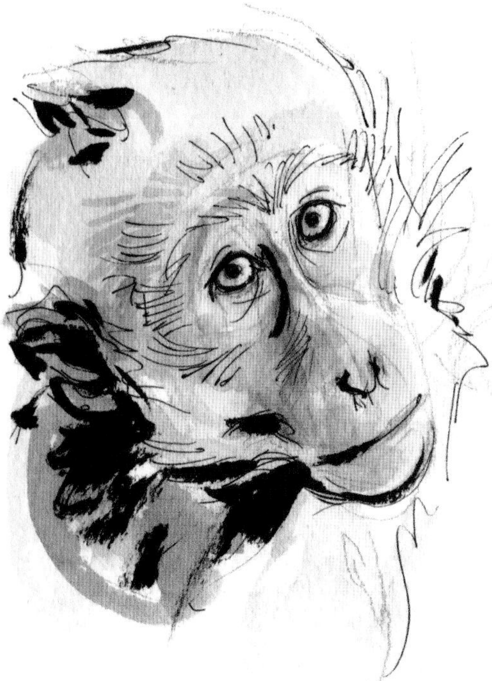

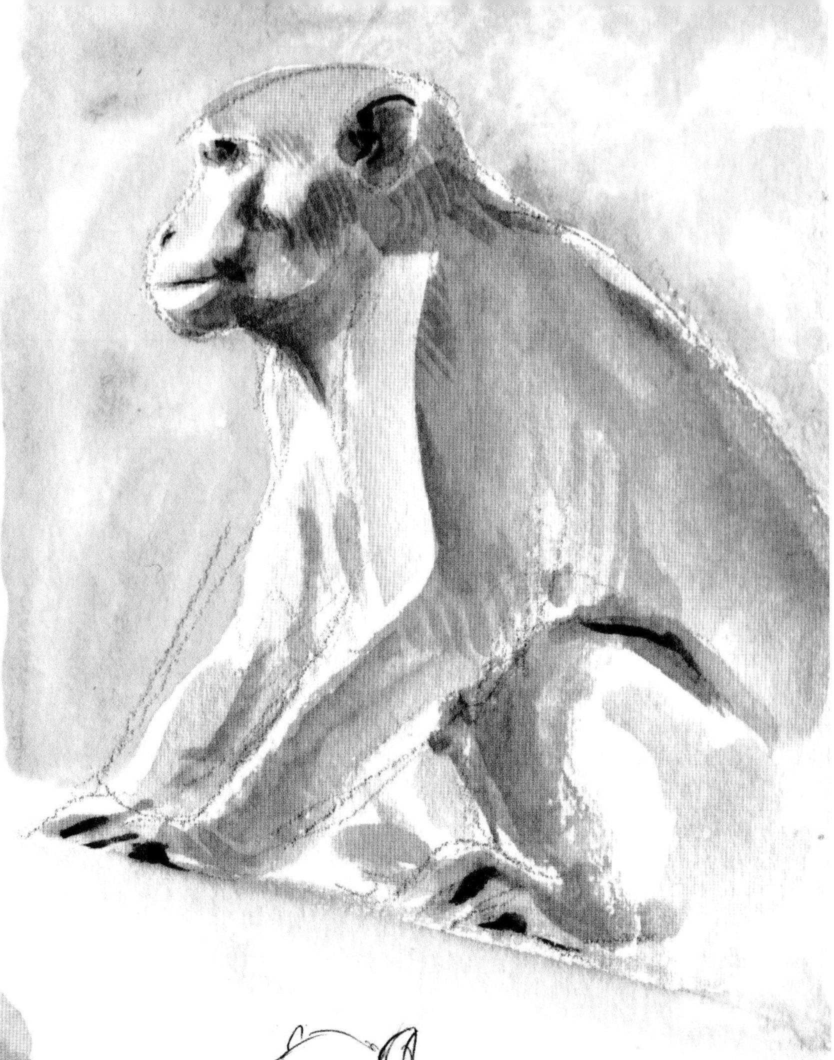

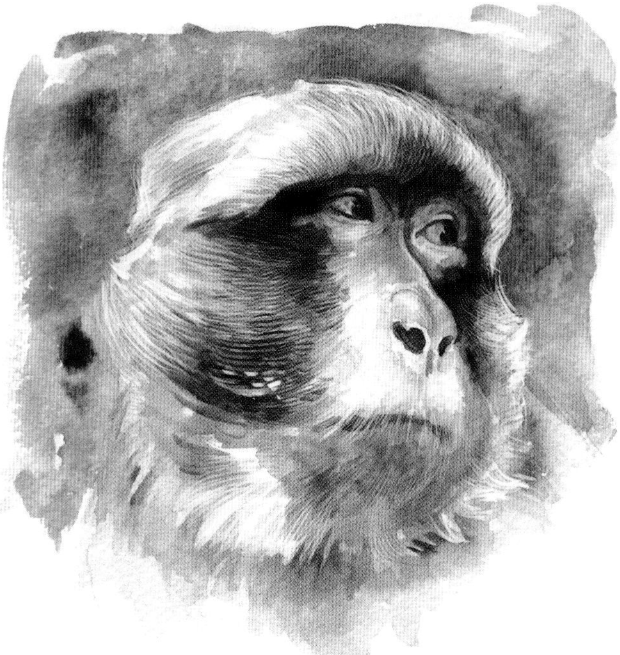

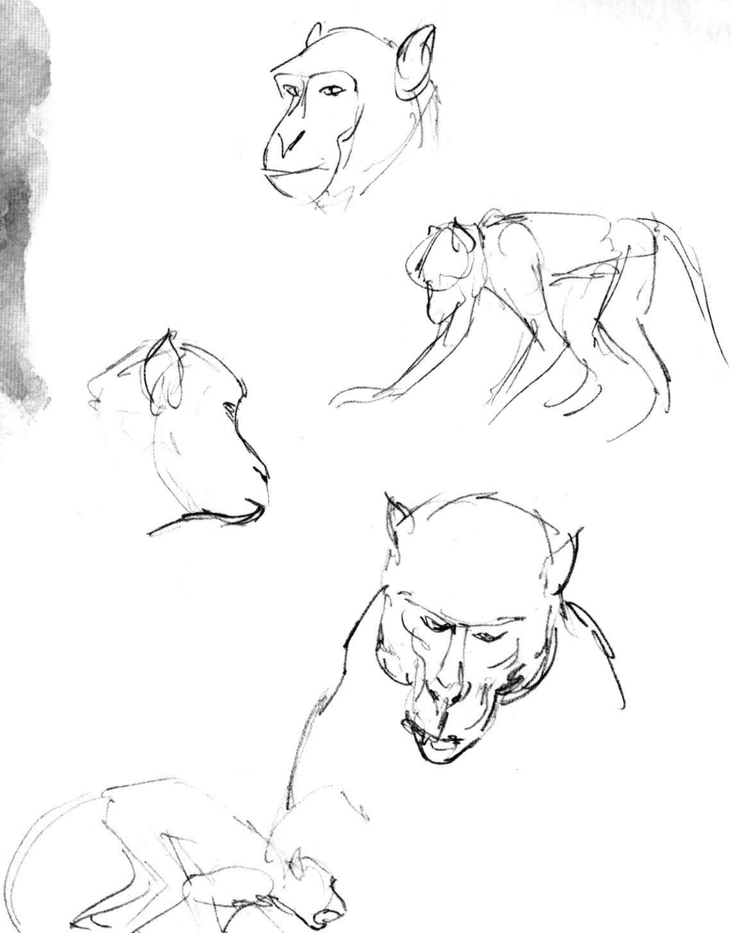

simius

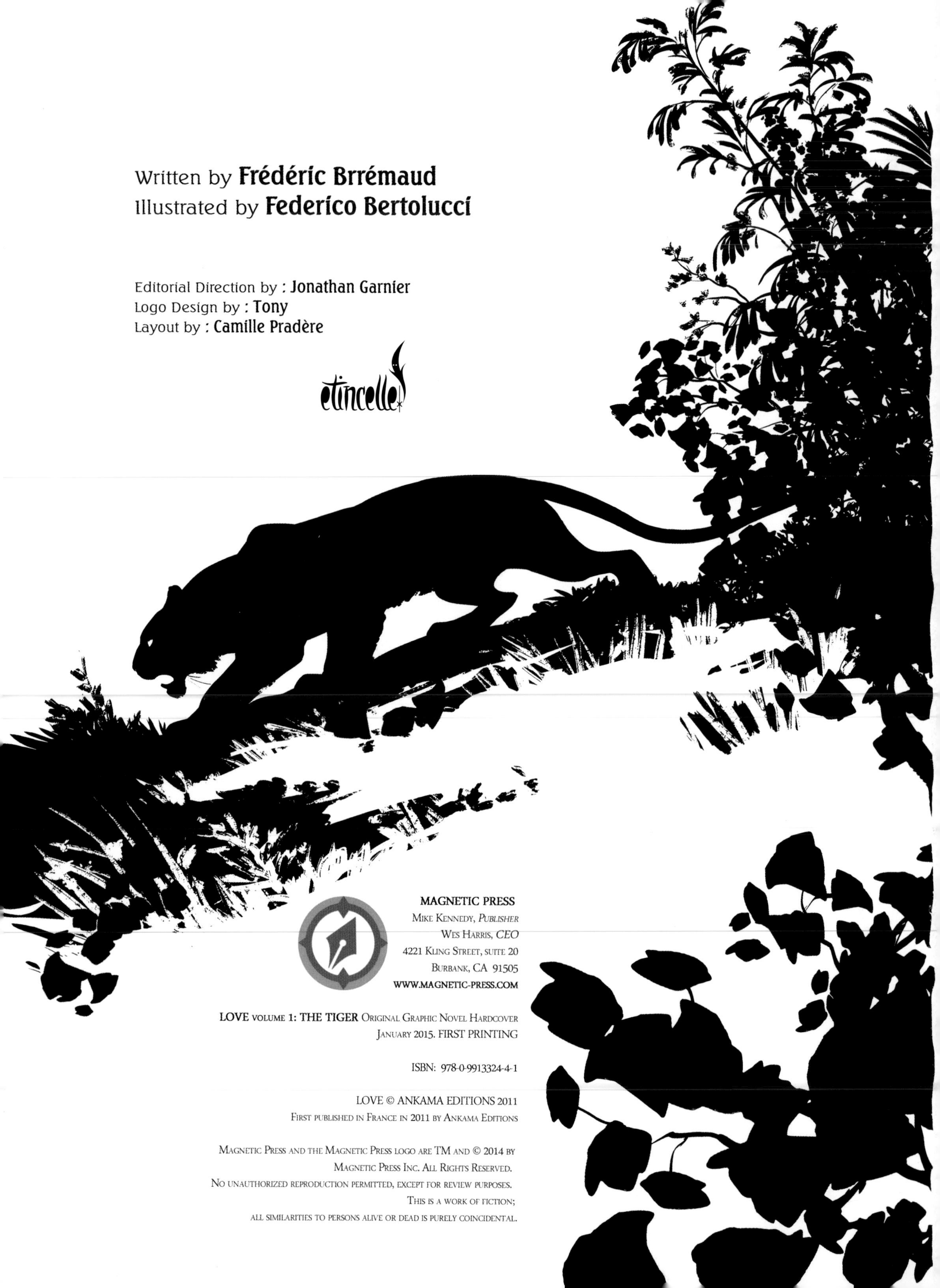

Written by **Frédéric Brrémaud**
Illustrated by **Federico Bertolucci**

Editorial Direction by : **Jonathan Garnier**
Logo Design by : **Tony**
Layout by : **Camille Pradère**

etincelle

MAGNETIC PRESS
Mike Kennedy, *Publisher*
Wes Harris, *CEO*
4221 Kling Street, suite 20
Burbank, CA 91505
WWW.MAGNETIC-PRESS.COM

LOVE volume 1: THE TIGER Original Graphic Novel Hardcover
January 2015. FIRST PRINTING

ISBN: 978-0-9913324-4-1